SECRETS
AND
LACE

(Fatal Hearts Book 1)

DORI LAVELLE

PROLOGUE

In his lifetime he had taken pleasure in many things, but nothing was quite as intoxicating as the marriage of blood and lace, the merging of red and white. This moment would be one he cherished forever, the moment that signified his first step toward correcting the wrongs that had been done to him.

He ached for more blood, and she had plenty of it. He slid the knife out of her body, plunged it back into her heart, and twisted the blade. It poured out of her as though from a hidden fountain within, soaking into the expensive fabric, staining what was once pure.

Excitement hit him like a bolt of lightning. He shivered. This feeling was so much better than sex, drugs, or alcohol. They said revenge was sweet. The bastards were right.

His eyes met hers and he grinned. Her tears drowned the shock and fear in her gaze.

It pleased him that she was terrified of walking through death's door. Fear of the unknown was worse than pain itself.

Tears trickled down the side of her face and dripped off the freshwater pearl in her earlobe. Her lips parted. She tried to talk, but blood gurgled inside her throat, preventing her from doing so.

"What's that? I can't hear you." He wiped a tear off her smooth skin, offering her a little comfort before she tumbled into the depths of death. "Shhh," he said. "It will all be over soon. Hell will welcome you with open arms."

Her body started to shake and her eyes widened, but there was no fight left in them. She was resigned to her fate. The moment he had been waiting many years for had come. Before his eyes, she went from a beautiful woman to a lifeless corpse...to nothing.

He inhaled the last bit of air that had exited her lungs and sighed with satisfaction. Then he swiped a palm over her eyes, shutting them forever.

His intention had been to punish her, to torture her until she begged him for forgiveness, but he had been unable to wait any longer. In the end, she died a beautiful death.

That was fine by him. Death was death. And she'd deserved to die.

CHAPTER ONE

I took a long sip of my champagne, the semi-sweet liquid prickling on the tip of my tongue before it trickled down my throat.

The *Sage* May issue we had all been waiting for had become a reality. My magazine had pulled it off yet again, unveiling a scandal that would have people talking for weeks to come.

Dane Mullin, a real estate mogul and media personality, had turned out to be a monster with a double life. We went to great lengths to blow the cover on his secret life in Mexico, where he had raped and impregnated an underage girl during a luxury holiday and was involved in a human trafficking scandal. In the end, he was caught with his pants down—literally.

Now, as *Sage* employees celebrated his humiliation and our success, Dane Mullin's face was on the cover of every copy. I had already gotten word that the magazines were flying off the shelves in every store in Boca Raton and around the country, and the phones were ringing off the hook as more and more advertisers tossed money our way.

Sage started off as a small online fashion and lifestyle magazine. I started it not long after I graduated with my Bachelor of Arts in Journalism and Media Studies—earned on a full scholarship from the University of South Florida—while working for a small magazine to help pay the rent.

Although I'd had a number of dedicated subscribers, I soon learned that safe topics only gave me a safe earning potential. I wanted to make the kind of money that would allow me to live the glamorous life I had always dreamed of.

With that knowledge, and plenty of confidence in my skills and talents, I took out a loan and jumped into the dark waters of scandal.

It paid off big time. The money flowed in, and I hired a staff of top-notch writers, editors, and photographers. My employees thought the way I did, and they didn't shy away from uncomfortable topics. The dirtier the scandal, the better. Sage was ahead of its competition in exposing the most humiliating secrets of people in the public eye.

Within seven years, circulation doubled, then tripled, making me a huge success at only thirty.

Now, taking another sip of champagne, I put

on a bright smile. I called for attention and all eyes turned to me. "You all did an amazing job with this issue. I couldn't have asked for a better team. Thank you for putting *Sage* on the map." I raised my glass. "To you all."

Andy, one of the photographers, shouted, "To Chloe Parker, the best boss anyone could have."

The room exploded with cheers and applause.

***

Once the champagne bottles were empty and the finger foods had disappeared, everyone except me returned to their offices to work on the next hit story.

After leaving the boardroom, I headed for the bathroom, careful not to trip in my six-inch Laurence Sabatini heels, focusing on taking one step at a time. It should have been my walk of success, the one I lived for after a major story hit the stands. I was well aware *Sage* was a weapon—one with the power to destroy lives. Our stories had led to countless arrests, broken marriages, and divided families.

From the outside, I was a successful, ruthless businesswoman. But no one saw the marks each issue left on my heart. Later today I would probably spot my magazine on a newsstand and find it suddenly hard to breathe, even as I smiled, walking by as if I owned the world.

I'd learned to tuck away my emotions and just chase the story. But when I was alone, a step back from my success, I allowed myself to feel small, to see the woman no one else saw. Not even Miles Durant, my fiancé.

With each new story I feared I would be exposed for the person I was, that I would be stripped of everything I had worked so hard for. I pictured my own face on the cover of *Sage*, my dirty laundry hung out for the world to see. Everyone would discover what a hypocrite I was. Each moment of success could be my last.

I opted for the third cubicle in the bathroom, the one farthest from the door. It would afford me a few moments of privacy as my mind took me back to my hometown of Misty Cove, Florida, the small town I left behind to go to college. I never looked back. After graduation, I moved from town to town, looking for the perfect place for me. Boca Raton was it. A new place, a new name.

I locked the door and leaned against it, eyes closed, heart thumping, sweat pooling on my forehead. I licked my dry lips, still tasting the expensive champagne.

I sank down onto the closed toilet seat and gripped the hem of my vintage Chanel black knit skirt. My eyes felt hot and fear knotted my stomach.

My phone vibrated inside my purse. I ignored it. It would be Miles congratulating me on yet another success, even though he'd made it clear he did not approve of what I did. He said the success of my magazine came at too high a cost.

Six months ago, he'd brought up, yet again, the subject of me giving *Sage* a new purpose: publishing stories that didn't ruin lives.

"Why do you have to find success in someone else's misfortune? Why publish dirt?"

"I don't understand why you keep bringing this up," I'd lashed out. "I've worked damn hard to get to where I am. The dirt I publish… that's my job, and I'm great at it."

"Only a heartless person could do what you do." Anger blazed in his eyes, so hot I felt it.

"If I'm so heartless, why are you with me? You knew what I did before we started dating."

That argument had been the worst in our six-month-old relationship. I thought at the time it would mean the end. But he'd surprised me by apologizing with a romantic dinner and a diamond ring. I had accepted his proposal and moved into his villa a month later, but I had never been able to forget the anger that had flared in his eyes. He was so passionate about stopping me, it had terrified me. That passion was what made me stand my ground. I loved him, but I wouldn't give up my career for any man.

In truth, as destructive as my job was, I didn't know how to stop. If I knew how, I'd let go, do something that didn't leave me feeling like crap at the end of the day. Chasing a good story was like a drug, a years-old addiction I had carried with me since high school when I was editor of the school paper.

I had everything, but success wasn't quite what it was cut out to be. At least it wasn't how I had imagined it as a child. Maybe it would have been if I didn't carry so many scars from the past.

I blinked away the tears. "Pull yourself together," I whispered, standing up on shaky legs. "This is what you wanted. This is your destiny."

In thirty days I'd have everything I'd dreamed of: a glamorous job, and a marriage to the perfect man. My place in the glittering world would be secure. I wouldn't let the past get in the way of my fairytale. It had seemed crazy, agreeing to marry Miles after only six months of dating, but it had felt so right to me. He felt right. Miles had wanted to get married within weeks of proposing, but I had insisted that I needed time. I only planned to get married once, and I wanted to do it right. I would need time to plan the perfect wedding.

CHAPTER TWO

"Chloe, wait!" Jolene Holyfield, my assistant, hurried toward me as I unlocked the door to my office. "Someone left this on my desk. It's for you." She smiled as I took what looked like a card and turned it over in my hand. "Maybe it's an RSVP for your wedding."

"Thanks, Jo. Maybe it is. See you at the meeting." I opened the door and walked into my office, still gazing at the card. Only my name was typed on the ecru envelope. No address. Why would I be receiving an RSVP in the mail? Everyone was asked to RSVP online, or to send physical wedding-related mail to Silk & Petals, the wedding planning company we had hired to plan the festivities.

My office, like the rest of the *Sage* offices, was decorated in pastel colors and swathed in lots of natural light. A vase of white roses stood on one corner of the smoky glass–topped desk. I crossed my legs under the table and moved my computer mouse so the screen came alive.

A photo of me and Miles was splashed across the screen, taken inside the Stephansdom last month in Vienna, Austria.

Work swallowed me immediately, and I forgot about the card. I returned a few emails—most from people congratulating me on the explosive issue—and returned calls. Later in the day I had a routine meeting with the team, and a successful lunch meeting with a big cosmetics firm.

At six, I was ready to leave the office—unusual since I tended to be the last person to go home. But I had a wedding dress fitting to attend. The wedding boutique was a few blocks down the street, so I walked. Tina Daly, my wedding planner, was there waiting for me.

The fitting didn't take long. My taffeta trumpet wedding gown, which had hand-beaded lace appliqués adorning the shoulder straps, fit as though it had melted onto my body.

Afterward, Tina went through details with me at a nearby café, where I sipped fizzy water from a crystal glass. The alcohol from the office celebration was still in my system.

"Do you know yet if your mom will be attending the wedding?"

My stomach twisted. That was one question I wasn't ready to answer yet. Honesty was the only way out. "I still don't know. Can I get back to you on that in a few days?"

"Sure, no problem." Tina closed the silk-covered wedding folder. "I guess that's it for today. Everything is going according to schedule. I've confirmed with all the vendors, and the wedding program is ready. It's gorgeous. You'll love it. I'll send you a copy." Tina's hazel eyes sparkled, a perfect match for her personality.

"Thanks so much, Tina. I'd appreciate that."

We parted outside, and Tina walked away with the folder under her arm and her auburn ponytail swinging like a schoolgirl's.

As I walked back to the office to get some paperwork I had forgotten, exhaustion pressed down on me. Even with a planner, wedding planning was stressful. Eloping would have been easier. But what was the fun in that? When I married the hottest bachelor in the country, I didn't want the world to miss it. And one of my writers, Lauri Brandon, had already started writing our love story, which would be published in the July issue, supplemented with wedding photos. Some good news for a change.

When I exited the office building again, a black stretch limousine was parked out front. I forgot about my meltdown in the bathroom earlier and smiled as Ed, Miles's driver, beckoned me over.

"Good evening, Miss Chloe. Mr. Durant

instructed me to pick you up this evening."

"That's lovely. Thanks, Ed." He opened my door and I slid into the back seat. The paperwork could wait. This evening was for Miles and me.

A bottle of champagne was chilling in a silver bucket, and a pair of classic fluffy white bunny slippers awaited me, a note tucked inside one of them.

After a long day, I thought you might need these.

Times like these often made me wonder what I did to deserve Miles. He was so thoughtful and loving—the most romantic man I had ever dated. He made sure to spoil me every chance he got. Although I was thrilled to be marrying a billionaire, I knew he'd be a keeper even without the money.

I kicked off my heels as the driver pulled away from the curb and pushed my toes into the slippers, sighing with relief.

The smile was still on my face when I leaned my head back and closed my eyes, imagining myself on my wedding day, admiring myself in the mirror before the ceremony, my shiny black hair glossy and beautiful. Happiness would banish the shadows of the past that lurked in my bright blue eyes the moment before I walked into my own personal fairytale.

***

I found Miles in the kitchen, cooking dinner.

We had a chef, but Miles loved to cook. It helped him relax. Whenever he was able to get away from his stressful tech company, he switched off his phones and stepped into the kitchen. That suited me fine, because I wasn't much of a chef. In fact, I hated cooking.

"How's my gorgeous fiancée doing?" He pulled me into the circle of his arms, and I pressed myself against his tight chest, feeling his hard abs under his crisp white shirt. He wasn't wearing an apron; how he managed to keep food from staining his shirt was beyond me.

He tipped up my face and pressed his lips against mine, sliding his tongue into my mouth, forcing my lips open. A shiver of desire rippled through me as I stood on tiptoe. He ran his fingers down my back, chasing the tension of the day from my body. I let go, allowing myself to be seduced by the only man to ever give me an orgasm.

Unable to stop myself from moving on to the next base, I raised my hands and buried them in his thick dark brown hair, my fingertips caressing his scalp. He lowered his hands to my butt and cupped me firmly, drawing me even closer, pressing my lower body against his rock-hard erection, awakening my senses.

He pulled away and looked into my eyes, his dark eyes sparkling with mischief. "Want to make this the first course?"

"I do." I giggled and rubbed myself against him.

His lips touched mine again, hungry and fast. In a few ragged breaths, I was up on the marble kitchen island. His pants were down, my lace panties were on the floor, and he was buried deep inside me. I moaned and groaned into his shoulder and he grunted in response.

It didn't take long before I came, as if he was all I had been waiting for all day. When we were done, my silk shirt clung to my body, and I was tingling between the legs, still feeling him inside me. It took a while for the pounding of my heart to quiet.

He helped me down off the island and I straightened my clothes. He pulled up his pants, kissed me on the nose, and returned to the stove. "The second course will be ready in ten minutes."

"Yes, sir. I'll go and change." I turned and went up the sweeping staircase, walking down a long corridor to our bedroom. I undressed and took a quick shower in the master bath. Ten minutes later I was back downstairs, still wearing the slippers Miles had left me in the limousine. I was refreshed, satisfied, and happy. I pretended to be happy at my job, but with Miles, I never had to pretend. As long as he was around, I was okay. This part of my life was real.

Later that night we made love again before Miles fell asleep in my arms. I was about to close my eyes when I remembered the card Jolene had given me at work.

I got out of bed, careful not to wake Miles, and went to my home office. I stared at the envelope for a long time before I opened it. It was a card, but definitely not an RSVP. This one had the number 30 embossed on the front. I opened the card and something slid onto the polished wooden table. My gaze landed on a piece of lacey material, and my heart stopped when I saw the red stain.

Blood.

The card fell from my hands.

CHAPTER THREE

I was panting by the time I reached Jolene's office door. I raised my hand to knock, then paused and swiped the sweat off my forehead. It wouldn't be a good idea to make Jolene suspicious.

I took a deep breath before pushing the door open and pretended my heart wasn't in my throat, where it had been since last night.

Jolene glanced up from her computer and smiled. "Morning, Chloe. Are you here for your appointments? You received quite a few calls this morning already." Jolene reached for a spiral notepad and started flipping through it. She located the page she was looking for, removed it, and handed it to me. I took it, forcing my hands not to shake.

"Thank you." I swallowed hard. "By the way, who did you say delivered that card yesterday? The one you found on your desk."

"I have no idea. I went to tidy the boardroom… and when I returned, there it was, next to my cashews."

I eyed the ever-present glass bowl of nuts on Jolene's desk.

"You didn't leave anyone in your office?" Visitors who entered the premises always booked an appointment. No one showed up unannounced.

Jolene frowned. "No. The next appointment wasn't due for another hour." Jolene narrowed her eyes. "Is something wrong? What kind of card was it?"

I forced a smile and gave a small nod. "Yes, everything is fine. You were right... just an RSVP."

"I'm sure you'll be getting a lot of those—" The phone rang and Jolene's eyes darted to it.

I gave a dismissive wave of my hand. "Go ahead and answer. Please hold my calls for the next thirty minutes, though. I have a few things to take care of." I reached for the door handle and walked out.

Inside my office, with the door locked behind me, I sat at my desk for a long time, thinking. The person who had left me the card had not wanted to be seen. What kind of person would go as far as sending someone a piece of bloody lace? Then again, the nature of my job meant I had a few enemies. Beyond that, I was about to marry one of the wealthiest men in the United States. There could be lots of people who might want to sabotage my happiness.

Unable to think about work, I pulled out the envelope. I'd stuffed the card back inside last night. I turned the envelope over in my hands, feeling the weight of what was inside.

In the end, I picked up a sheet of paper and made a list of everyone I knew who might want to hurt me. But when the list of names reached twenty, I crumpled up the paper and tossed it into the bin. Furious at being left in the dark, I pulled out the card and the piece of lace and put them into the shredder.

Maybe someone was playing a tasteless prank on me. I decided to stop worrying about something that might be nothing at all. I wouldn't mention it to Miles. No use worrying him unnecessarily.

I got to my feet and went to the decorative mirror hanging on one wall, where I ran a brush through my hair and refreshed my plum lipstick. I would be a professional and go through my work day under the pretense that I had never received the stupid card.

I called Jolene to tell her to allow my calls through. I was available.

Three hours later, I had my first meeting of the day. Although I did an amazing job of pretending, I was a total mess inside.

I could not stop picturing my own eyes when

I'd looked into the mirror earlier. The fear in them had been unmistakable, fear of a kind I remembered all too well from long ago. The body could lie, and words could be deceiving, but eyes were the windows to the truth.

CHAPTER FOUR

If only a shower could wash away more than dirt.

I had been standing under the chrome shower head for almost an hour, trying but failing to scrub away the things that terrified me. As I walked out of the bathroom, followed by a cloud of steam, I felt the same as I had when I went in earlier. I'd thought a shower would do me good, but it did nothing.

I unraveled the towel from around my head, and my black hair tumbled down my naked back in ropes of silk.

Miles walked in, followed by the usual invigorating scent of cedar, citrus, and musk. He looked distinguished in a traditional black tux with prominent satin lapels. It gave him the kind of class and appeal only he could pull off. He was clean-shaven, and his medium-length chocolate-brown hair had been lightly gelled and combed back, the lines softened by him running his fingers through. He looked both clean-cut and ruggedly handsome at once, and my heart quickened as I watched him.

He glanced at his Rolex and then at me with a pinched expression. "I thought you would be ready by the time I got home."

I sighed. If I didn't hurry up, we could end up having an argument over something as silly as being on time. I made a mental note: *Don't show up late at the wedding.*

"The event starts in twenty minutes. Ed is already waiting outside."

I dried my hair while walking into my wardrobe. "Come on, Miles. What's the big deal? It's just a fundraising event. We'll get there on time."

"It's not *just* a fundraising event, Chloe. You know how important these events are to me."

One of the reasons I fell in love with Miles was because he cared so much about the less fortunate—the sick, the poor, the misunderstood. He not only went to philanthropic events to show his support; he left each one with his pockets thousands of dollars lighter. Sometimes he even got his hands dirty serving soup and handing out donations to the homeless.

Many times, though, it *did* annoy me that he took these events so personally. And we were always going to one or another. We rarely went out just to have fun, not like we used to when we'd just started dating. I didn't mind donating money, or attending a charitable event now and then, but two to three times a month seemed like a bit much. But then, I knew about this side of him when we got together. I signed up for this.

While I dressed, I heard him shuffling around in the bedroom. He was pacing. I'd have to do my makeup in the car. I got the feeling he was on the verge of walking out the door and leaving me behind.

Normally I didn't mind his strict adherence to time so much, but today I wasn't in the mood. I'd even tried to get out of attending, but it was important to him that we show up as a couple, to show our joint support to the community.

"I'm almost done," I called out, massaging rich lavender lotion into my arms. I needed a massage badly; I'd have to fit one in soon.

Ten minutes later, I emerged dressed in a long, strapless silver and black evening gown with sequins that blinked when I moved. I didn't have enough time to do my hair the way I had planned, so I dried it and pulled it back in a smooth low bun.

By the time I put on my shoes and picked up my clutch purse, Miles was already out the door.

The drive to the Boca Raton Resort & Club

was quiet as Miles read through emails and talked on the phone, all the while holding my hand. When we arrived, he kissed me on the lips and told me I was beautiful. My earlier annoyance dissipated as we stepped out of the car.

At least three hundred people were present at the AIDS Gala. Owen Firmin, Miles's best friend and former business partner, was among the people in the room.

Both Owen and Miles had studied computer science and mathematics at the University of Florida, but they ended up developing Torp Mobile, a popular social app that made them both wealthy. They had gone on to grow what later became the company Torp Inc., a corporation that earned Miles—its president—the title of top businessman several years in a row, according to Forbes magazine. The company had created several more apps since then, as well as other products. Miles was an amazing success and he wasn't even thirty-five.

Owen, who was a year older than Miles, had fallen by the wayside. The money had gone to his head. He was a party animal, not a businessman. Soon after I started dating Miles, Owen—whom I had disliked from the get-go—had been voted out by the other board members. Now he was free to do whatever he liked—which meant throwing money around, partying, and breaking hearts. He'd already had his story in an issue of *Sage*. Miles had been pissed, but I told him it was a business decision, and Owen was the kind of guy our readers wanted to read about.

Owen was a jerk, though. The last time I saw him, he'd come over to our house for dinner, and when Miles left the room, he tried to flirt with me. I was furious and threatened to tell Miles, but Miles was protective of Owen. And frankly, I didn't want to be the one to come between them. The one thing that still infuriated me was his insistence on showing me that he didn't think I was the right woman for Miles.

"Chloe, you look amazing, as usual. It's great to see you." Owen kissed me on both cheeks and I fought the urge to push him away.

He wasn't wearing his usual flannel shirts and jeans. Instead he actually looked handsome, with his medium-length dark blond hair slicked back and none of the five o'clock shadow he was so fond of on his face. His bright blue eyes sparkled from behind his glasses.

"Thank you, Owen." I forced a smile and reached for a glass of champagne off a tray carried by one of the waitresses.

We were shown to a round table near the front of the ballroom. Somehow, despite there being five people at the table, I was seated next to Owen. As the night wore on, I did my best to ignore him. Instead, I carried on conversations with Miles and some of the other guests at our table.

Speeches were made, and even Miles was called up to say something. He ended his speech with a heartwarming thanks to his fiancée for her endless support. He always did that—made sure everyone knew I was the lady by his side.

Dinner was served and I did my best to get through it with a smile on my face. Halfway through dessert, I excused myself to go to the ladies' room. I had to get away for a bit. Sitting for two hours straight doing nothing was exhausting. I wanted to tell Miles we should call it a night, but he was having such a good time. I'd wait another half an hour.

I used the toilet and refreshed my makeup. When I put my lipstick back into my purse, my spine chilled. Another ecru envelope was tucked inside my purse, similar to the one I received yesterday. The one I had shredded. This one was folded in half so it would fit inside the clutch. My fingers trembled as I pulled it out. Even though no one else was in the restroom, I locked myself inside one of the cubicles and sat on top of the toilet seat. I ripped the envelope open, knowing exactly what I would find, but wanting to make sure.

The card was identical. But this time, it had the number 29 framed by a gold border instead of 30. As I had expected, a piece of lace was tucked inside the card, complete with the red stain. This was no longer something I could sweep under the rug.

I pushed it back into my purse, feeling suffocated. The card had not been inside my purse earlier. That meant one thing. The person sending me the cards was at the event.

CHAPTER FIVE

The next morning, I continued trying to convince myself that the cards were part of a prank. Maybe the red stain on the lace wasn't even blood. It could be food coloring or paint.

My hopes crashed when, during my lunch break, I went to the ladies' room and did a test with hydrogen peroxide. I'd bought a small bottle on my way to work. I poured it on the piece of lace and it foamed up. My online research claimed it would if the stain was blood. But was it human or animal blood? On second thought, why did that matter? Sending someone fabric stained with blood, human or animal, was disturbing.

My eyes watered as I watched the liquid bubble up on the fabric. I wanted to look away, but I couldn't move, couldn't tear my eyes away. Now that my suspicions were confirmed, what should I do? Could I tell Miles?

I'd tried to tell him last night, going as far as waking him up in the middle of the night, telling him I wanted to talk. But at the last minute the words froze inside my throat. I ended up telling him to go back to sleep, that I only wanted him to know I loved him.

If he suspected it was someone seeking revenge for an article published in *Sage*, we would end up in yet another argument over my job. I didn't have the energy for that, and I didn't want to make things complicated when we were about to get married. On our one-month dating anniversary, Miles had told me I was a breath of fresh air, that the women he'd dated before had been too complicated and had come with too much baggage for him to handle. During our year of dating, my job was the only thing we fought about. If I told him about my stalker now, I might also have to tell him about the skeletons in my closet. I had lied to him for a year, or at least withheld important information. And I had lied to myself, thinking I could lead a normal, worry-free life. I had reinvented myself, blended in with the crowd, and fooled people into thinking I had a squeaky-clean image. The cards I was receiving proved I had not run fast enough from my past. It would only be a matter of time before I came face-to-face with it.

In a moment of stupidity and denial, I tore up the card and flushed it down the toilet, along with the piece of lace. I was well aware of the fact that I was destroying potential evidence. I could've presented it to the cops. But cops were among the people I could not talk to about this. They would ask me who wanted to harm me, and they had the resources to dig into my past, to dig up skeletons I preferred to stay buried.

But keeping this information to myself was as damaging as letting it out. I needed to talk to somebody. Someone I could trust. The first person who came to mind was Kirsten Bannister. Since moving to Boca Raton, I had kept most people at a distance, never forming close relationships. If I wanted to keep my past out of sight, I couldn't get too close to any one person. The more people I let in, the more ways I allowed myself to be exposed.

Apart from Miles, Kirsten was one of the people who managed to climb over the wall I had erected around myself, although she, too, didn't know much about my past. I told her the same thing I had told Miles: I was born and raised in Misty Cove, Florida, but I had not gone back since I left for college. I *did* open up to them about my nonexistent relationship with my mom, but that was about it. I made sure they focused on the new me, and I brushed off as many questions about my past as possible. They thought they knew me, but they had no idea.

I first met Kirsten five years ago when I was

out for a jog. We had bumped into each other several times, as we jogged the same route. We got to talking and met up for coffee, which led to many more. She was a good listener, and a good friend. The kind of person I needed right now.

***

"Are you okay?" Kirsten sipped her café au lait, her hazel eyes suspicious. "You seem preoccupied." She stopped talking and waited for me to respond.

I was overwhelmed by the urge to back out at the last minute, to keep my troubles to myself. But bottling everything inside was unbearable.

"I think somebody's stalking me." I pinched my lips together.

The blood drained from Kirsten's face. "What do you mean? What makes you think that?"

I drew in a long breath and told her about the last two days, the two cards.

Kirsten shook her head, her straight red hair swaying like a curtain. "Who would do such a thing?"

"I wish I knew." My heart lightened. Sharing my predicament with somebody else helped a little, even though I couldn't tell her about the possible connection to my past. I stirred my hot chocolate and licked the spoon. The sweet taste was soothing. As a child, Mom used to make me hot chocolate every time I was upset. That was before she withdrew from me. Before she became somebody else.

"I thought maybe it's a prank." I gave a nervous laugh. "Maybe the person will get bored soon and leave me alone."

Kirsten drained her coffee and put the cup down. She leaned forward across the table. "Are you kidding me?" Her voice was a furious whisper. "This is not something that will blow over on its own." Her words were firm, and her hair swayed with each word. "This is not a joke, Chloe. When a crazy person sends you blood through the mail, you call the cops. You take the evidence to the police; you don't destroy it."

I understood. If I had been somebody else, with a different life, the police station would have been my first port of call. I would've filed a complaint the instant I discovered it was blood on the lace.

My earlier relief dispersed when it dawned on me I had made a mistake by telling Kirsten. She was my friend. Of course she would be worried and urge me to go to the cops. And I had no way of explaining to her why I couldn't go, not without her becoming suspicious, and asking questions I didn't want to answer. "I think I should wait. It could be nothing. Given the nature of my job, I'm pretty sure things like this happen all the time. We don't hear about it often, because stalked people might not always run to the cops."

"But you still shouldn't have destroyed the evidence, just in case."

Kirsten was two years younger than me, but sometimes she acted like a big sister. "I guess I wasn't thinking straight. I was just... scared. I thought if I destroyed it, it would go away." I chewed the corner of my lip. "Do you really think the person is counting down to my wedding day?"

"It looks like it. I mean, what are the chances somebody would send you a card with the exact number of days before your wedding on it? I have a bad feeling about this."

"Okay, I think I'll wait and see what happens over the next few days. Then I'll decide what to do. I promise not to destroy the cards. But maybe I won't even get a card today."

"I think that's unlikely." Kirsten pulled her purse into her lap and removed her wallet. "Someone who sends you blood is not only sick; they could be dangerous." She inclined her head. "Do you think maybe someone wants to blackmail you? The whole town—heck, the whole country—knows you're engaged to Miles Durant. Maybe they saw an opportunity to make money? Maybe you should tell Miles. He could pay them off so they leave you alone. The truth is, cops can be slow sometimes."

I had not considered blackmail before. Up to this point, I'd thought the person was trying to scare me. I was almost relieved, but my thoughts reminded me that blackmailers often used a piece of nasty information they had on a target to get what they wanted. Blackmail or not, the end result would be the same. I couldn't get Miles involved. And I couldn't confide in Kirsten any further... at least, not about this. I was alone."

CHAPTER SIX

When I arrived home in the evening, I found a note on the bed from Miles. He'd gone on a last-minute business trip to Miami. He didn't say when he'd be returning, and his phone went straight to voicemail.

"Did Mr. Durant mention when he'll be back?" I asked Mary, our housekeeper.

Mary looked up from polishing the silver and smiled, shaking her head. "No, ma'am."

"Thanks, Mary." I went back to our bedroom and had a shower. The jet of hot water beating down on my head and shoulders did nothing to relax me.

My mind spun. Even though I kind of regretted opening up to Kirsten about the cards, it had still made me feel better to share the news with someone. During my drive home, after a lot of back-and-forth, I knew I had no choice but to tell Miles. I'd told Kirsten, and she was so worried about me. What if *she* told him? I'd asked her not to, but fear made people do things they didn't plan on doing. I should know that.

If Miles found out I didn't go to him first, he'd be hurt. So I'd tell him the exact same thing I told Kirsten; nothing more.

I stepped out of the shower and pressed a button at the corner of the LED wall mirror. The steam coating it melted off as if by magic, leaving it crystal clear.

For a long time I stood on the thick bathmat, naked, dripping, studying my slim but curvy body, my eyes, my hair.

For the first time since leaving Misty Cove thirteen years ago, I felt like that girl again. The girl I used to think was ugly, with the tasteless clothes and chubby cheeks. Now I had designer clothes, expensive makeup, and a great body, but my eyes... The fear that had clouded them through my first years of college and beyond had turned them from, golden honey to deep maple syrup. And there were dark bags under them now.

I raised my hand and placed it on my heart. It vibrated with each rapid beat. Vomit rushed up my throat and I ran to the toilet, making it just in time. Snot and tears mixed as I retched.

I couldn't even remember the last time I'd cried. I'd come to be quite good at holding back the tears, even when hurting. So many things had happened in such a short time, things that had changed my life and scarred me forever. Things that had happened because of decisions I had made. Those dark memories I had tried so hard to ignore were rushing up, and they rendered me helpless to fight them.

After a long, good cry, I brushed my teeth and washed my face. Then I draped a fluffy towel around my body and left the bathroom. Though my sobs had quieted, the tears kept coming, streaming hot down my cheeks. My chest ached as it had that night thirteen years ago. I could keep the truth from the world, keep my scars out of sight. But the layers I had wrapped around myself were starting to peel away.

It was before nine, but I climbed under the covers anyway. I normally worked or read a book before falling asleep. And since Miles often got home late from work, I liked to wait up for him, for his arms to wrap around me when I fell asleep.

Tonight, I lay on his side of the queen-size bed, hugging one of his pillows tightly. I searched for his smell, his comfort, but couldn't find it. Mary had already washed the sheets and pillows. Washed away the familiarity.

For the first time in a long time, I felt alone. Even though I didn't get too close to many people, I still had a lot of friends. Most of them had entered my life after I started dating Miles, which wasn't a surprise. If I picked up the phone, there would be someone on the other end, willing to meet up for a coffee or a movie. But unlike Kirsten, most of those people were little more than acquaintances. If they knew who I really was, they would be gone in the blink of an eye.

***

When the doorbell rang at 10 p.m. I was still awake, soaking Miles's pillow with my tears. Who would visit this late? I was not in the mood to entertain anyone, and my eyes and face were sore and puffy from crying.

I lay there for a few minutes, praying whoever it was would go away, but the doorbell wouldn't quit. Mary had already gone home, so I had to go to the door. My body ached as I climbed out of bed and put on a robe. I made a quick stop in the bathroom, where I quickly splashed my face with cold water, dabbed concealer on the bags under my eyes, and squeezed drops into my eyes to lighten the redness. The result wasn't amazing, but an untrained eye would be fooled into thinking I was just tired.

While the doorbell continued ringing, I put on jeans and an oversized t-shirt, pulling my long hair into a messy ponytail on my way out the door. As I descended the steps, I hoped the person had given up waiting and left. No such luck.

Owen, wearing jeans and a blue flannel shirt, stood at the door, his whole weight pushed against the doorframe. I recoiled from the smell of alcohol drifting off him. He was far from the well-dressed gentleman I had seen at the AIDS Gala a few days ago.

"What are you doing here?" I considered not letting him in, but I wouldn't be able to close the door with him blocking it. He didn't look like he had any more energy left to move. I moved aside and he almost fell into the house, catching himself in time. I closed the door but didn't lock it. I would never lock myself in the house alone with him.

"I need a drink." He stumbled toward the bar in the downstairs living room. He picked up a bottle of gin, unscrewed it, and took a long swig straight from it.

Disgust roiled in my stomach and I grabbed it from him. "I think you've had enough alcohol tonight."

No wonder he had been pushed out of Torp. Who would want to work with him? He was a mess. I wouldn't put it past him to show up drunk at the office.

The decision to let him go had weighed on Miles. Miles had mentioned that Owen had been missing work, showing up late for meetings, even bringing random women to the office. After leaving Torp, Owen threw a fit that lasted for weeks, but eventually they made up.

Since leaving the company, Owen had pursued his passions:

women and booze. He had no shortage of girlfriends. Even without a job, he had the looks and the money to make women fall at his feet.

Owen stumbled onto one of the couches. He attempted to sit upright, but kept folding to one side. "I want to talk to Miles." He pointed an unstable finger at me as I stood under the chandelier.

"He's not here, Owen. He is in Miami. Call him and ask when he'll be back, then come and see him." I shivered when I remembered the second card, the one I discovered at the gala. "What do you want from Miles, anyway?" It had to be important for Owen to show up at our house so late.

"None... none of your business." He fell onto the couch.

"It *is* my business. It got me out of bed." My breath came quick and sharp. Almost gagging at his stench, I sank onto the leather chaise lounge.

"Owen, what is it you have against me?"

Owen looked up then, appearing almost sober. For a few seconds his blue eyes cleared and drilled into mine, causing a chill to race down my spine. "I have plenty of reasons not to like you, Chloe. One of them is your stupid gossip magazine that got into my business."

"You wouldn't have ended up in *Sage* if you'd lived your life more responsibly." Even as I said it, I wondered: Would he end up telling me the same thing one day?

He pulled himself up with difficulty. "You pretend to be so perfect, so put together. You know what? I think it's a cover... for something. You make other people's lives your business." He cleared his throat. "I wonder if somebody looked into yours what they would find. Would you qualify for a feature in your own trashy magazine?" He lowered himself back down.

"So, you're the one... the person sending me those cards? The lace?"

Owen groaned in response. I couldn't tell whether his answer was a yes or a no because he was snoring now, black-out drunk.

I'd gotten enough information from him to raise suspicion. I wouldn't be surprised if it was him. I had to find out the truth. If he was the one, I'd be forced to tell Miles.

CHAPTER SEVEN

I found Owen's phone on the dashboard of his Maserati, but it was switched off.

A quick glance at the front door assured me he was probably still asleep. He had been too far gone to even stir when I'd removed the keys from his pocket.

I pressed my thumb on the power button but the phone remained dead. Shit. I let the phone fall into my lap.

Feeling sick and frustrated, I pressed my fist to my forehead and squeezed my eyes shut. When I opened them again, I froze. Owen was outside the car, a confused expression cutting through his drunken haze. How had I not heard him open the front door?

My breath hitched inside my throat and my knees knocked against each other. Before I could think of what to do or even come up with an excuse, he yanked the door open, standing in my way so I couldn't exit the car.

"What do you think you're doing?" His voice

was controlled and cold, matching the sadistic smile that cut across his face. It was no longer laced with alcohol. "You do know you're in the wrong car, right?" He opened the door wider and his eyes narrowed. "Is that my phone? Were you going through my things, Chloe?"

He reached into the car and picked the phone up from my lap, glanced at it, and then back at me with what could be described as a look of triumph. "I always knew you couldn't be trusted. Looks like I was right." He moved aside. "Get out."

I got out of the car, my cheeks burning, my knees trembling uncontrollably. I was both embarrassed and angry at myself for getting caught red-handed. "I was..." I breathed in to collect myself. "Look, you were asleep. I needed something from—"

"My car? What could that be?"

I couldn't come up with an answer. "I... Nothing. I have to go."

Owen slammed the car door closed and leaned against it, arms crossed across his muscular chest. The light coming from the moon and standing lamps in the driveway made him look menacing. I took a step back but he grabbed my wrist, his strong hand tight around it. "I find you in my car and you think you can walk away without an explanation?"

"Let me go." I yanked my hand from his grip

and massaged it. I had to face him head on. He could be the only one to give me answers. "It's no secret that you don't like me. The feeling is mutual. I know you don't want Miles to marry me. But to go that far? What you're doing is considered a crime."

Owen narrowed his eyes. "And it's not a crime to break into someone else's car? Or are you above the law?"

"Stalking someone is much more serious than looking for something inside a car that's on my property."

"Wow." He rubbed his strong chin. "That's what you think of me...?" He got into his car, slammed the door, and leaned his head out the open window. "I was wondering how long it'd take you to figure it out. Yes, I've been looking into your past. If you had succeeded at switching on my phone, you would have found a dozen Internet searches about you and your life before Miles. You're not as untouchable as you think." He held my gaze. My eyes burned. "Watch your back. One day you'll pay a high price for messing with people's lives."

Before I could say anything more to defend myself, he started the car and drove off, tires screeching.

As furious as I was at him, a trace of worry fluttered in my heart. He was driving on alcohol and anger. What if he had an accident? Owen was like a brother to Miles. Miles would be devastated if anything happened. I pushed the thought out of my head. Right now I had to worry about myself. Owen had pretty much admitted he was the person stalking me. And his parting words held an unmistakable warning.

My suspicions grew even more when I returned to the house and found another card in my walk-in wardrobe. Had he put it in there while I was outside, or had it been there earlier? I had no way of knowing; I had not been in there since getting home from work. Instead of giving in to my fears this time, rage rushed through me. Who did he think he was? I'd worked too damn hard to get where I was. I would not let him ruin my life.

I knew that an Internet search about me wouldn't yield any results. I did such a search at least once a month to see if anything from my past had popped up. Till now, a search of my name only returned information about *Sage*, and my relationship with Miles. Owen was only trying to scare me—he didn't know my real name. At least, not yet. I had to get Miles to stop him before he dug something up.

I picked up my phone from the bed to call Miles, and a missed call from him was displayed on the screen. He'd left a message that I should return his call.

My stomach was in knots as I waited for him to pick up. It rang several times with no answer, and I almost ended the call when his baritone voice came on the line. Tears welled up in my eyes. I missed him so much and suddenly wished he were home, holding me.

"Sweetheart, hey, are you all right? You sound like you're crying." His voice was gentle and warm, which made me cry even harder.

I blew my nose and shook my head, as if he could see me do it. "When are you coming home? I need to talk to you."

"Is something wrong? Is it to do with the wedding?" He sounded concerned.

"No." I pinched the bridge of my nose. "It's to do with me. Something's going on and I need to discuss it with you." I tried to control myself, but the crying wouldn't stop. I'd never felt more out of control. The weaker side of me was pushing its way to the surface and I was helpless to do anything about it. It brought along with it all the insecurities I thought I had left behind.

"I have a business meeting in the morning with the Vendet Group, the tech company I told you we're in the process of merging with. I planned on being home for dinner." He paused. "But you don't sound fine. Go to the airfield. I'll arrange for someone to fly you out with the second jet. It's Friday... maybe we can stay until Sunday, turn it into a little romantic weekend."

It took me a while to respond. Flying to another town would require more energy than I had at the moment. But I also couldn't talk to Miles about this over the phone. And I needed to be with him right now, in his arms. I took a deep, steadying breath. "Okay, I'll pack a bag."

CHAPTER EIGHT

It was 11:30 p.m. when I soared into the night sky, holding on to the envelope I had found inside my wardrobe. In a way it was a good thing that I had found another card. I was about to accuse Owen of stalking me. Nothing spoke louder than physical evidence.

It wasn't long before I stood in the spacious elevator of the Marwood Hotel, my hands still clutching the envelope and the handle of my bag as I headed for the deluxe suite where Miles stayed every time he was in town.

Being in Miami always reminded me of the early days of our relationship. Since Miles had so many business contacts in Miami, and I had been unable to get enough of him, we'd spent a lot of time here.

I had loved staying at the Marwood with him; it was one of the taller buildings in town and had a great view of the skyline. I had felt like an excited girl as he twirled me around the private living room. We had made love everywhere in the suite—the oversized closets, the huge bathrooms, the king-size infinity bed, and even on the thick wool carpets.

I looked forward to more quality time together like that, and a break from work. Starting Monday, I wouldn't be going back to work until after we returned from honeymoon. I hadn't taken a day off in months.

Miles was at the door waiting for me, wearing black pants and a custom-made gray shirt without a tie. The large oak writing desk at the far end of the living room was scattered with papers and I suspected he hadn't stopped working all day. He was as much of a workaholic as I was.

"How are you doing, my love?" He kissed me, pulling me into a hug and into the room. I trembled in his arms. Coming to him felt like coming home. He closed the door with his foot and continued holding me tight.

I pulled away and looked into his eyes. "I'm so happy to see you." Before I lost my nerve, I decided to get right to it. I walked over to one of the couches and dropped my bag and purse onto it, lowering myself down. Miles came to join me, questions in his eyes.

"You're not having cold feet, are you?" He gave a nervous laugh, and then his smile faltered when I didn't smile back.

"No, I don't have cold feet." I took his hand

into mine and squeezed it. "I love you; I want to spend the rest of my life with you. I've never been more sure of anything before."

"Should I get you something to drink before you tell me what's going on?"

"No, I'm okay. I had a glass of wine on the jet." I pulled my hand from his and turned to face him. "The past few days have been kind of difficult for me. Miles, I think somebody's blackmailing me."

"What do you mean somebody is blackmailing you?" His eyes darkened.

I reached for my purse and pulled out the envelope. I removed the card and the piece of lace fluttered out, dropping to the carpet between my feet. My gaze followed it and I watched it for a moment.

Miles bent forward and picked up the lace. He held it between his forefinger and thumb, his brows knitted. "Is this... It's not what I think it is, is it?"

"It is. It's blood." I handed him the card. "Someone's been sending me these. It looks like a countdown to our wedding." I took the card from him again and showed him the number on the front.. "I received this one tonight. I... I tore up the first two." I looked at him, searching his face for a reaction.

"Three days? Why in the world didn't you come to me with this earlier?"

I threw my hands in the air and let them drop onto my lap. "I don't know. I thought maybe it was a prank."

Miles reached for the card again and turned it over and over in his hand, as though looking for some hidden message. "This can't be a joke." He shook his head while holding my gaze. "You should have told me—we could have gone to the cops."

I made a prayer gesture with my hands, pleading with him. "I thought if you knew, you would connect it to my job. I didn't want us to fight."

"Of course, that's exactly what I think." He shot to his feet. "This must have something to do with your job. Someone you featured must want revenge."

I buried my head in my hands. "I think you're wrong." I looked up at him again. "Miles, I think I know who it is." I allowed the words to settle between us.

"Well, who?" Miles shook his head in confusion. He tossed the card back on the couch.

I hesitated before saying anything. The last thing I wanted to do was get between Miles and Owen. I didn't want to force Miles to take sides. What if he didn't take mine? "I think—I *know* it's Owen."

Miles walked across the room to the desk

and picked up a glass of water. He drank it in one gulp and turned back to me with his hands in his pockets. "That's ridiculous. Why would Owen do something like that?"

I stood up and went to the large windows, gazing out into the night, not appreciating the view this time. "You know as well as I do that he doesn't like me. I don't know what he says about me to you, but he's made it clear to me that I'm not the right woman for you." I turned around, my arms folded across my chest. "He came over to the house a few minutes before I called you. He was drunk and passed out. I thought I'd look at phone to see if I could find something, any kind of evidence that he's involved." I stopped talking and wrung my hands.

"Go on." Miles went to sit on the couch again. "What did you find that confirms he sent you the cards?"

"Nothing. His phone was dead. He found me trying to switch it on."

"So you didn't find any evidence. Just because he hasn't warmed up to you doesn't mean he would do something so drastic."

My chest ached. Miles was on Owen's side. "He said some things that made me suspicious." I bit my trembling bottom lip. "But it's not just the things he says to me, it's the way he says them. He implied that I might pay a high price for what my magazine does to people."

Miles didn't say anything for a long time, just sat there looking at me. What was going on inside his head? Was he agreeing with Owen? "You know what I think?" he finally said. "I'm pretty sure there are many people out there who want revenge for having their life stories splashed across the cover of a gossip magazine for all the world to see. You invade people's privacy. Do you know how many people you have hurt by exposing their lives?"

I sat down as anger rose up my throat. "So you think it's my fault this is happening? You know what I don't understand?" I shook my head in dismay. "You knew what I did for a living when we met. Why are you even with me?"

Miles ran a hand over his hair. "I love you. That's why—even though I don't like what you do for a living. I know the lengths people are willing to go when they're hurting. I live in constant fear for you." He waved the card in the space between us. "This just confirms my fears."

"Some of the people *Sage* exposes have done really bad things. People get attacked in the papers all the time. I haven't heard of any becoming stalkers."

"I don't care about what other magazines

do." He reached out and pulled me to him. "You're going to be my wife. I don't want to spend sleepless nights wondering if somebody's out to get you."

"I don't think you have to worry about anything. I told you that. I think this is a one-off. And I know you hate to hear it, but my gut tells me Owen has everything to do with it." I gazed into his face. "Can you at least talk to him about it? Tell him to stop?"

"You do understand what position you're putting me in, right? Accusing my friend of something so atrocious?"

"I'm your fiancée, and I'm afraid. I know this is uncomfortable for you, but I thought I would be your priority."

He placed my head between his hands and kissed me on the lips. "You *are* my priority. That's why I'm against what you do. I'm trying to protect you."

"And what I'm saying is that my job might have nothing to do with this." I pulled away from him and stood up. "I'm telling you it's Owen, and you're defending him. How do you think that makes me feel?"

"Fine. I'll talk to him in the morning." He clasped his hands together. "What if it *is* him? What then? Will you go to the cops?"

"No." I shook my head. "He's your friend. I wouldn't do that to you."

"Let me ask you another question. If it's not Owen, what will you do?"

I sighed. "I think it is him."

"Come here." Miles reached his arms out and I walked into them, but his embrace didn't give me any relief. He had chosen Owen over me. That hurt.

"Promise me something," he said into my hair. "If Owen has nothing to do with this, we'll go to the cops."

Tears burned my eyes. I held on tighter to him, afraid to lose him. He would never understand why I didn't want to get the cops involved.

"Promise me," Miles repeated.

"I promise," I lied. I had already made a decision. If I got another card, I would not tell Miles—not until I got to the bottom of this by myself. If it turned out Owen was innocent, I knew the place to go looking for answers. Much as it pained me, I'd have to go home, back to the place where my fears were born.

CHAPTER NINE

Over breakfast in bed on Saturday morning, Miles gave Owen a call and put the conversation on speaker.

As I had expected, Owen denied everything. He threw a few curses over the phone for both Miles and me. Then he told us to fuck off by dropping the phone.

"Great," Miles said angrily, and tried to call him again. The call went to voicemail.

We finished the rest of our breakfast in uncomfortable silence. Miles didn't have to say a word as he finished his eggs Benedict and then got ready to go to his meeting with the Vendet Group in the hotel conference room. It was obvious he was angry with me for driving a wedge between him and Owen.

"The meeting should be two hours at the most." He fastened his cufflinks. "I think it's best we return home once I'm done."

I nodded, my heart crashing. The romantic weekend had been canceled without my consent.

In a way I felt guilty for accusing Owen. I had known him for a year and he had made threats before that had amounted to nothing. When Miles mentioned the piece of bloodied lace to him, he had been furious.

Even though the knot was still tight in the pit of my stomach, I had to make things right with Miles. We would be getting married in a few weeks. This was not the time for us to be fighting. We should be excited about our wedding.

I went to help him with his tie. "Good luck with the Vendet Group." I kissed him. "I'll come home with you, but I'll only be passing through to get my car and some more clothes. There's someplace I need to go for a few days."

"Going on a wedding shopping spree?"

I smiled bitterly. "No, I already have everything I need. You and Owen still need to go for a last fitting, though."

"I'll do that first thing on Monday. So, where are you going?"

"Home...to Misty Cove."

Miles cocked an eyebrow. "That's a surprise. I thought you never wanted to go back there."

"I know. But it's time. There are some things I need to take care of."

"I guess it's not a bad idea for you to get away from whoever is sending you those cards.

I still think you should go to the cops, though."

"I'll go to the cops if I get another card."

"Good." He kissed the side of my neck. "I'll come with you if you *do* go."

CHAPTER TEN

The sun was setting when I arrived in Misty Cove. Holding my breath, I turned onto Broadridge Road, the one road leading to my childhood home from out of town. If there were any way I could avoid it, I would have. But I had no choice but to drive right through. If only I could close my eyes and drive blindly until I reached my destination.

Five minutes into my drive along the road, it started to drizzle. As soon as I turned on the wipers, the drizzle turned to gushing rain, the drops lashing against my windshield and roof. The sheet of water obscured the road, making it hard for me to see where I was going.

Had I been superstitious, I would've thought something was trying to stop me from coming home. If I could still call Misty Cove that. After a few minutes of trying to make my way through the storm, careful not to veer off the road, I slowed down and pulled off, parking on the shoulder. I'd wait it out until the rain subsided or I'd end up in a ditch somewhere.

Through the sound of the rain hitting glass and metal, the pounding of my heart still made itself heard, loud and clear. I wished I were anyplace but here.

To distract myself, I turned on the radio and cranked up the volume. Classical music poured into the car, drowning my thoughts. I closed my eyes and tried not to think, telling myself that even though I felt like the old me, chubby Kelly was gone, and I was Chloe, the beautiful, successful businesswoman. But the little voice inside my head told me I'd always be Kelly, the desperate girl who had done everything she could to fit in.

My phone rang and I picked up on the fourth ring.

"I've been trying to reach you all day. I hope everything is all right." Tina already had a naturally soft voice, and I strained my ears to hear her over the rain.

"Sorry I missed your calls. I'm out of town. I'll be back in Boca Raton in two or three days. Is it urgent?"

"No, not really, I was finalizing the seating charts, and I remembered that you still hadn't gotten back to me about your mom's attendance. Should I count her in?"

I took a few deep breaths to calm my racing heart. One of the things I would have to face in

Misty Cove was my mom. We had not talked for thirteen years, and I didn't look forward to seeing her. When I'd turned ten, she'd suddenly pulled away from me. While my bond with my father had been unbreakable, she became a stranger. There were times I even thought she was jealous of my close relationship with my father. And when my father died, she didn't offer me any kind of comfort. What kind of mom was jealous of her own child?

But could I really come to town and not see her? In a small town, I wouldn't be able to pretend I didn't see her if I bumped into her. I'd spent the last thirteen years pretending she didn't exist, but how could I do that here?

"I'll let you know in a couple days." I changed the subject. "Did you manage to pick up my dress?"

"All taken care of. The seating chart can wait. Give me a call when you know."

"Thanks. And Tina, I'm taking a few weeks off from work. Starting Monday, I won't be in the office until after the honeymoon. I'll only be available on my cell."

"Got it."

Fifteen minutes later, the rain died down, and I was able to hear myself breathe. I started the car again.

When I drove past a bed–and-breakfast, it occurred to me that I had not made any

60

accommodation arrangements. My childhood home wasn't an option, not after all that had happened. A hotel would be the better choice for now.

Driving through the small town, past pastel-colored cottages, I was glad most people in Misty Cove were already in their homes. It was the kind of town that slept early.

I stopped at a small four-star hotel ten minutes from Misty Cove High School. I would've preferred to stay at a hotel farther from my old school, but I was tired and wanted to sleep. A small thirty-something-year-old woman with two thick braids and equally thick glasses stood behind the counter at reception. She was so engrossed in her dog-eared novel that she didn't look up when I approached. I waited for a moment, pretending to be interested in the old, framed road map on the wall behind her. Then my annoyance flared.

"Excuse me. I'm sorry to pull you away from your book, but I need a room."

Her head snapped up. "I'm so sorry." As she observed my face, her face froze. It was clear she recognized me instantly, though I struggled to place her familiar face. How was she able to see past my much longer and straighter hair, my slimmer figure, and the expensive makeup and clothes and still see the old Kelly?

"Oh my God," she exclaimed, releasing the

smell of chewing gum. "Aren't you... Aren't you Kelly Pearson? You look so different." She stretched out her hand for a handshake. "We went to school together. I'm Jenna Simons."

I shook her tiny hand without meeting her eye. "Of course, Jenna. Yes, I remember you." Memories flooded back. Jenna had been one of those girls who didn't give a damn what anyone thought. She hadn't cared about clothes or makeup and spent pretty much every lunch break in the school library. We had been so different. I'd been a complete people pleaser, had ached to belong, to be seen. "How have you been? Nice to see you again," I lied, plastering a smile on my face.

"Same here. It's been years. You never came back after leaving for college. I heard you even changed your name. I can understand why, though. In your position, I'd probably have done the same."

Her words stabbed me in the stomach.

"Yes, it's Chloe Parker now. I've been traveling a lot." I would leave it at that. I didn't owe her, or anybody, an explanation. I was here for one reason, and then I'd be gone. This time they'd never see me again. "I'm not in town for long. Do you have a room for the next three nights? A suite, preferably." I handed her my credit card.

"Wow, fancy." Jenna smiled and glanced at

her computer screen. "Living the high life, are we?"

Was that envy I heard in her voice? Or was it my imagination?

I decided not to respond to the comment. I had nothing to apologize for. I enjoyed staying at expensive hotels, and I could afford it. While I was here in Misty Cove, I'd stay in a suite and not feel guilty about it. High school was a long time ago.

"Yes, our suite is available. Here's your card, and here's information you might need." She handed me a keycard and a small folder. "Your room is on the fourth floor. Breakfast is between 8 and 11 a.m. Lunch starts at 12:30. If you need anything, call down."

I appreciated her professionalism. "Thank you so much." I picked up my carryall bag and headed for the elevators. I looked forward to climbing into bed. I needed to tank energy for the next few days.

When the elevator doors opened, Jenna called out to me by my old name. I turned back, wondering if I had forgotten something.

She leaned forward across the counter as though wanting to whisper something to me. "People around here haven't forgotten that last article you wrote for the school paper, and, you know... what happened after. They still talk about it. Just be prepared."

Sweat beaded at my temples. The next few days were going to be harder than I'd thought.

CHAPTER ELEVEN

My phone was ringing when I got out of the shower.

Kirsten was breathless on the other end. "Are you screening my calls?" she asked, but I could tell from her tone of voice that she was joking.

"Now, why would I do that?" I inspected my nails. They were in need of a fresh coat of my favorite opaque blush polish. "What are you doing, anyway? You're breathing so hard it's almost hard to hear what you're saying."

"I'm on the treadmill. I need to look my best at your wedding. The whole country will be watching."

"I don't think you need to lose weight. You have an awesome figure."

"I agree." She laughed, and then her breathing slowed down. She must have stopped exercising. "I'm just making sure it stays that way. So, where the hell are you?"

What would it hurt to tell her? Even if she knew where I was, it would be impossible for her to know my reasons for being here. "You won't believe where I am." I unraveled the towel on my head and the warm, damp ropes of my hair hit my naked back. "I'm in my hometown."

"Wow, that's a surprise. You never said you were going. You went to see your mom? What made you change your mind about seeing her again after all these years?"

"I came here to take care of something else. But now that I'm here, I'm kind of thinking it would be weird if I don't drop by to see her, don't you think?"

"Maybe she's not the same person she used to be. Thirteen years is a long time to stay the same. But it must be hard for you to be back there."

"Yes, it is." It would be damn hard to face my mom again. Thinking about her made it hard to breathe. What would we say to each other? Where would we start? How would I be able to look past the pain? "Kirsten, I'm so sorry, but I have to go. Do you mind if I give you a call later?"

"Sure. Go and do what you have to do. But when will you be back in town?"

"I don't know yet. I'll be here for two more days, probably. Though it could be a little longer." I had no reason to rush back, especially since I didn't have to be in the office. But I couldn't stay away for too long either. The wedding planners would want me to sign off on a number of things. The wedding would be my main priority once I returned to Boca Raton.

"Well, okay." Kirsten paused. "I had wanted it to be a surprise, but since you don't know when you'll be back, I guess I have no choice." She sighed. "I've organized a bachelorette party for you for Wednesday."

"You did? You're such a sweetheart. Thank you so much." I had been so preoccupied that I had not even thought about a bachelorette party.

"What else are maids of honor for?"

"In that case, I'll try to make it home by then." Today was only Sunday. I'd have enough time to find the answers I needed. After that, I saw no point in staying in a town that was no longer home to me.

"Is everything ready for the wedding?" Kirsten asked. "Not much time left."

"Pretty much. Tina called yesterday. She's finalizing the seating charts. She seems to have everything under control." After Miles proposed, I had considered planning the wedding myself, being involved in every moment leading up to my special day. But I soon realized that wedding planning was lots of work that I didn't want to do. It was Kirsten who had convinced me that delegating the planning to someone else wouldn't make the day any less special. And besides, there was one thing I would not be able to delegate: the moment at the altar with Miles when we exchanged our vows.

Kirsten had even been the one who suggested Silk & Petals. A client of hers had apparently used them before.

"That's great. If there's anything you'd like me to take care of while you're out of town, let me know."

"Thanks, Kirsten. I'll do that. Talk to you soon."

I ended the call and spent a long time getting dressed, worrying about seeing my mom again. It would be best to visit her first, to get it out of the way before getting to what I came to Misty Cove for. I'd keep it short. I had no interest in rehashing the past, talking about what had driven us apart.

Before I left the room, I gave Miles a call, hoping he would help calm my nerves. He was in church, but he stepped out to talk to me. Although he was surprised that I'd be seeing my Mom, he didn't try to talk me out of it.

Miles was Catholic, so as long as he wasn't traveling, he never missed Sunday mass. It was something he carried with him from childhood. His late mom always took him with her. I did find it a bit painful that it was a part of his life he didn't seem to want to share with me. I wasn't Catholic, but I believed there was only one God, served in various ways.

At the start of our relationship, I did accompany him once or twice, and while he had not objected, he did give off the vibe that he wasn't so comfortable with me around. It hurt a bit, but I took a step back. He had the right to spend some time alone, to recharge. At the end of the day, he came home to me. Nothing else mattered.

I walked out the door of the hotel feeling confident, telling myself I would be able to handle whatever came my way. My future with Miles was secure. All I had to do was iron out the kinks that had recently shown up, and then I'd be able to start a new life with the man I loved.

CHAPTER TWELVE

Misty Cove had barely changed. Before going to my childhood home, I drove through the streets for a few minutes, taking a look around, curious to see what had stayed frozen in time.

Turns out, almost everything. The Sunset Cinema I had gone to as a child had been replaced by a bed-and-breakfast, the Candy Cane sweet shop was now an ice parlor, and the Sneak and Peek video store had a "for sale" sign across its front door. Everything else was unchanged. It was almost like I'd gone back in time. Even the sounds and smells were the same.

The ocean sounded different here. It was the one thing I missed; it had soothed me so much during hard times. I had spent endless hours on the beach, collecting shells or gazing out at the ocean, wishing the waves could wash me away from my life. In Boca Raton, my life was so hectic that I often forgot to stop and listen to the ocean, and even when I did, it lacked the soothing effect I had experienced in childhood.

Mixing with the sound and smell of the ocean, the aroma of freshly baked bread and spices snuck through the open window of my car.

It was amazing how some things could change so much, while others stayed the same. Had Misty Cove awaited my return, waited for me to give it a second chance? I heard it calling out to me, trying to lure me out of the car, to walk its streets and gaze through its shop windows like I used to.

It felt like only yesterday when I'd last gazed through the floor-length windows of Mary Jane, a clothing store for teens, visualizing the clothes on my own body, showing them off at school. Sometimes I *did* gather up the courage to go inside. I tried on the clothes to see how they felt on my skin, dreamt that one day I'd be able to buy all the beautiful things I wanted.

My parents had bought me what I had needed, nothing more. My father was a struggling car salesman for most of his life, and Mom had been a housewife. After my father died, Mom got a job at a local bakery that didn't pay much. After bills were paid and the necessities bought, there'd been hardly enough money left over for extras.

I was still thinking back when I pulled the car onto Clover Avenue. It had remained the same as well. Rows of jacaranda trees still lined the street, and Andy's Grocery was still there, its bright yellow paint peeling. I watched as early grocery shoppers walked in and out, carrying bags, pushing carts, or holding tight to toddlers' hands—carrying out their morning tasks.

The Handy Car Wash was still at the end of the street, and as usual, the place was deserted. Most car owners preferred to wash their cars themselves to save money. I had always wondered how they had managed to stay in business with only a handful of customers. Rumor around town was that Jake Simpson, the owner, was in the business of money laundering, and the car wash business was a cover.

I pulled up in front of my childhood home and parked. I climbed out, of the car and for a second I stood there, the sunlight spilling onto my head and shoulders. Today was such a nice day, so promising after the storm that had raged last night. I wore a baby blue chiffon print dress with an open back and a pair of beaded sandals. The air was clean and fresh, the heat of the sun warm against my back.

I tipped my head back so I was gazing at the upstairs bedrooms, locating the one that had been mine, nestled between my parents' bedroom and the guest room.

The curtains were different. The purple ones

I remembered from my childhood were gone and replaced with boring beige ones. My stomach churned. I had moved on and so much time had passed. What if Mom had moved out? Maybe the house belonged to someone else now, a new family that would be able to fill it with laughter.

The living room curtain fluttered. Someone was peering out, but they didn't want to be seen. I moved forward and opened the metal gate. As I walked down the stone path, I clenched my fists tight, one of my hands holding the car keys and the other my phone. My stomach roiled.

I made it to the front door and took a deep breath.

I pressed a finger on the black doorbell, forcing myself to remain calm.

When the door opened, a stranger stood before me.

CHAPTER THIRTEEN

Mom had not moved out, but she was far from the woman I used to know. The sunken eyes, pale skin, and thin hair were nothing like what I remembered of the woman who had given birth to me, the woman I had loved until she stopped loving me back. Her hair had always been so beautiful, lustrous and thick, and I had envied her for it. I had dull hair growing up, but now, with a little help from expensive hair products and frequent visits to my hairdresser, it was as beautiful as Mom's had been at the time, if not more.

We stood there staring at each other—familiar strangers. Neither of us knew what to say or do. My heart shrank as I reached deeper into her eyes. Instinct urged me to turn around and leave. Nothing left for me here. I had done what I'd planned. I'd seen her. Now I could leave, right? There was only one problem: I couldn't move or speak, or even breathe.

"Kelly." She gripped the doorframe. "You're

home." Her voice was low, and it seemed the words were hard for her to speak. Before I could respond, she reached out and wrapped her thin arms around my neck, sobbing into my shoulder.

***

Mom didn't speak again for a long time. Neither did I. I was in complete shock over what had just happened.

I had not even planned on entering the house; I'd thought I would say hello to her and be on my way. I had not expected her to invite me in. But here I was, following her inside.

What had happened to her? Why was she suddenly being nice to me? Why did she look so withered?

She waved a hand at the faded, flowery couches I remembered and I took a seat, crossing my legs.

The TV was the same, the one I had been so excited to help my father pick out at the age of eight. I had never imagined it would end up being a major part of my life, the ultimate distraction from my home life. TV and lots of books. I eyed the film of dust covering the screen and looked away. Dust was everywhere else I looked, however; it covered the old radio, coated the dead leaves of the houseplant on the windowsill, and even my Mom's beloved collection of ceramic figurines.

Although I didn't mind a little dirt here and there, Mom always had. She had been obsessed with cleanliness it drove me crazy. She had cleaned house all the time—in the mornings, afternoons, and even after I went to bed. The sound of the vacuum cleaner was unbearable. That was why I bought the quietest vacuum cleaners money could buy.

Mom sat down in the armchair that had belonged to my father. Even in the same room, the distance between us was great. So many hurts, so many unspoken words.

"I'm so glad you're here. I dreamed of you last night. I had no idea it was because you were coming home today."

I cleared my throat. "I just came to tell you that I'm in town to take care of some things. I thought you might want to know." I clasped my hands tight so they wouldn't tremble. Why was I even explaining anything to her? What was I doing here in the first place? She hadn't been a mom to me for years.

Mom shrugged. "It's nice of you to stop by." Her sunken eyes didn't leave my face. Was she afraid I would disappear again? Why did she care? "You look lovely... so different."

"Thank you." I swallowed hard. "You look different, too."

"I know." Mom tugged at one of her dry strands of hair. "A lot has changed since... Tell me, how have you been?"

"I've been okay...busy."

"Dan Mullot from the post office mentioned a while ago that he saw you in a magazine. You've changed your name. "

I nodded, feeling guilty. "It was a business decision. He must have seen me in a copy of *Sage*, my magazine."

"Kelly wasn't fancy enough for you?" Something flashed across Mom's features—disappointment, pain, regret?

"I like Chloe better." Was she seriously trying to make me feel guilty for the decisions I had made, the person I had chosen to become? What right did she have? "I'm not here to fight. I just came to tell you I'm in town and that's it." I attempted to stand up, but Mom raised a hand to stop me.

"Please," she begged. "I'm sorry, I didn't mean to make you feel bad. I've missed you so much. I prayed every day that you would come back to me."

A bubble of anger formed inside my throat and burst before I could stop it. "That's strange. I'm surprised you even noticed I was gone. I thought you'd be glad. You never wanted much to do with me when I was here." I sucked in a breath. "In fact, as I recall, you chose your boyfriend over me. Even after what he tried to do to me. You didn't believe me. You took his side. Now you want me to believe you've changed?"

Mom stood and came to kneel at my feet. She looked up at me, tears trickling down her cheeks. "I'm sorry for everything, Kelly. I made so many mistakes, and I can't take them back." She wiped her eyes with the back of her hand. "I know you thought I didn't love you. But I did. I really did love you. I love you… so much. I just didn't know how to show it."

"How could I have known you loved me?" My own eyes welled up. "I needed you, but you were never there." I remembered the exact day Mom started pulling away from me. At my birthday party. One moment she was there, singing happy birthday, asking me to blow out the candles and make a wish. And then she went to the bedroom to get the presents she had bought for me. When she returned, she was acting strange, no longer interested in celebrating. During the days that followed, I'd tried to believe it was a phase that would be over soon, and then we could return to our normal lives. The phase never ended. It lasted years, taking me all the way into high school and out of it.

"Kelly—"

"Chloe. That's my name now."

"Okay." Mom sniffed. "Chloe, there's so much you don't know."

"I'm sure there is." I blinked back tears.

She gripped my knees. "Please let me explain. I want to tell you everything."

I didn't say anything, just leaned back and folded my arms in front of my chest. My fingers were sore from being clenched so tight earlier.

She buried her head in my lap. "On your tenth birthday, everything changed for me. One minute I felt like the luckiest woman alive. I had a beautiful daughter and a husband I adored. A husband I thought loved me back. That day when I went up to get your presents, I found a note in your father's suit jacket." She cried harder. "It was from a woman. It was intimate."

I clenched up inside, but I refused to move, to think, to breathe. I waited for what I knew was coming: more news to destroy the only happy part of my childhood.

"I was so broken I didn't know how to act. I asked your father about it...later." She lowered her head. Her gray hair was more concentrated on her crown. "He didn't deny the affair. He'd been sleeping with one of his customers for over a year. After all the years I had been there for him, he cheated on me. He slept with someone else while I was at home preparing his meals and washing his clothes. He destroyed everything I believed about marriage and family. He destroyed me."

My chest tightened and guilt burned my

insides. How could I not have known? How did I miss her pain?

And how could my father, my hero, do something like that?

I wanted to pretend it wasn't true, but Mom wouldn't accuse my father of something so horrible just to get close to me, would she? Deep down, I knew she was telling the truth. All those fights they'd had in the middle of the night. I'd thought they had been fighting about me. I thought my father was angry with her for pulling away from me. All this time, I believed it was her.

I placed a hand on her head, which grew heavier in my lap.

"We were separated for years. We lived in the same house and shared the same bed. It was all for show. He didn't want you to know the truth. You're the reason he stayed. He continued seeing the woman."

"Why didn't you leave?" I heard myself ask.

"I didn't want to destroy you... your childhood. But I still pulled back. Every time I saw you with him... I guess I was jealous that he still loved you and no longer loved me." She looked up, her eyes red and swollen. "I ended up destroying your life anyway. Your father wanted us to wait until you graduated from high school. He wanted a divorce. But he died before that happened."

I engulfed Mom in a hug, her pain soaking into me. "I'm so sorry. I'm sorry for everything."

Both of us cried. After a while, the air seemed to clear. It was as though most of the pain had been released, and all we had was a clean slate.

Mom got to her feet, wiped her eyes, and blew her nose. Then she gave me a broken look as she sat back down on the couch next to me. "I'm sorry I didn't believe you about Alex. I don't know what was wrong with me. It's just... he was the first man to show interest in me in a long time." She shifted. "But there's no excuse for what I did. He tried to rape you. I should have protected you." She took my hands in hers. "After you left, I *did* confront him." She gave a half shrug. "He wasn't the man I thought he was."

"You know what?" I wiped away her tears. "Let's move on. He tried, but he didn't succeed. I fought him off. I'd like to leave that part of the past behind. If that's okay with you."

"I just feel so bad. I don't think I will ever forgive myself. I wasn't even there for you when that scandal of an article spread like wildfire through town... and what happened to Mariela Jones. I was so angry with you for what you said about Alex. I wasn't there for you." She gripped my hands. "What you did was wrong, but you're my daughter. I should have been on your side no matter what."

"Mom, really. I forgive you. Don't worry about it." I had to tell her more about the article she had just mentioned, but right now she needed to know that our relationship was okay.

She tightened her grip on my hands and I felt the bones in her thin fingers. "Before we start over, there's something else you should know. Two months ago, I was diagnosed with brain cancer. Doctors say I have about six months to live."

Time stood still. I had just gotten her back, and now she was telling me I was about to lose her again?

For a while I didn't react visibly, didn't know how to. I stared at her like a zombie, my face growing cold as the blood drained from it. "How?" I asked when I rediscovered my power of speech.

"That was my first thought when Dr. Brian gave me the news. I couldn't believe it was happening to me, yet it was. I had to deal with it."

No wonder she had changed so much, become so thin and frail. Cancer had taken everything away from her. My stomach twisted when I realized I would never have known if I hadn't come to town. She would have died all alone.

"I'm so sorry. I can't believe this is happening. I can arrange for you to come see the best doctors in Boca Raton. Come and live with me...and my fiancé."

Mom's face brightened at my words. "You're getting married? I'm so happy for you, honey." She pulled me into another hug that left me breathless, then pulled back and smiled at me. I detected a flicker of her old self. "I feel much better knowing you have a good life."

"Thank you. But I want you to share that life. Come live with us in Boca Raton. Let me take care of you." I shrugged. "Who knows, maybe there's something that can be done."

She shook her head sadly. "It's incurable. No one can help me. It took me so long to come to terms with what is happening to my body, I just don't feel like I have the energy to start all over again. I don't want to give myself hope and have it taken away." She touched my cheek. "Honey, thank you for the offer, but I can't come and live with you. I've done enough damage to you. You deserve to live a carefree and happy life, the kind I was never able to give you. Just do one thing for me, if you can. Stay with me for the few days you're in town. Come home."

"Of course I'll do that. I'll get my things from the hotel in a bit."

"Thank you." She tipped her head to one side. "Can I ask what you came to Misty Cove for? If you feel comfortable talking to me about it."

I paused. Should I distance her from the pain of worrying about me, or start our new relationship by being honest? Instead of discussing my problems, I would have preferred to discuss her treatment options, to convince her to return to Boca Raton with me. The last thing I wanted was for my problems to affect her. But she looked so expectant, waiting for me to respond.

I took a deep breath and closed my eyes. "Mom, I think I'm in danger."

CHAPTER FOURTEEN

My gaze wandered around the room, which was lit up by the bright morning sunlight filtering through the lace curtains. The curtains were the only new thing in my childhood bedroom. Mom had kept everything else the way it was before I had left. Even though she had neglected the rest of the house, she had kept my room clean. No dust or cobwebs in sight.

I felt horrible when I thought again of what she had gone through. How I had walked out of her life without knowing the full story. We had lost so much time together. I should have talked to her before leaving. Instead I had secretly applied to colleges without her knowledge and packed my bags. I couldn't get out of Misty Cove fast enough.

Then again, she wasn't the only person I had wanted to run from.

My gaze took in a poster of a blond teenage girl in a bikini—Mary Lewis, a famous singer back then. I remember putting up the poster, wishing I were her. Desperate for her looks, and her fame and fortune. Last I'd heard, the pressures of success had led Mary Lewis to the grave early. She'd overdosed on pills two years ago.

I climbed out of bed and went to the wardrobe. The multicolored butterflies were still stuck to the door. I had been drawn to butterflies as a child, an attraction born of the wish to be free, to fly away. Wishes *did* come true, but sometimes at a high cost.

The door squeaked when I pulled it open. The shelves and drawers were empty. Mom must have packed up my clothes and put them in boxes in the basement. An image of the way the wardrobe had looked with clothes inside pushed its way to the forefront of my mind— folded and arranged according to color. Through high school, the colors had evolved from dull and gray to colorful and bright. They had changed along with me. One moment I had been an invisible girl, the one who wore oversized and shapeless clothes to hide her unflattering figure. Until everything changed, and I was suddenly the girl everyone wanted to hang out with. My clothes and style changed along with my popularity.

The thing that had thrown me into the spotlight was the school newspaper. My articles had made waves, especially my column, StudeX, which was focused on revealing interesting facts about students' lives, and sometimes exposing secrets. Since nothing was off-limits, before the column was launched, interested students had to sign a release form to be considered for a feature. They'd had no control over what would be written about them, and the journalism was done undercover. The sheer number of signatures we'd received had been astounding. The StudeX column went on to change some of my fellow schoolmates' lives—along with mine.

I walked over to my desk, listening to the sound of vacuuming coming from downstairs. I bit my lip as I ran a hand over the pile of schoolbooks, and the old computer on which I had completed so many of my articles and homework assignments. The tips of my fingers brushed the scars in the wood of the desk. I noticed a tiny heart in the upper left-hand corner. *Larry loves Kelly*.

Larry had been *that* guy. The one every girl wanted to be with and every guy wanted to be. He was captain of the football team and just about the smartest guy in school. Coupled with his muscular chest and good looks, it was a killer combination. I'd pined after him all through high school, but I never thought he would notice me. Until he asked me to be his prom date. That was after my final StudeX feature, the one that made me the most talked-about girl on the last day of school. It also made me enemies. Secretly, I hated myself for what I had done, but the success had numbed the guilt, just as it did now with each new *Sage* cover story.

Before going downstairs, I gave Miles a call. I hadn't been able to reach him last night.

"I have good and bad news," I told him when he picked up. "I'll start with the good news.

"Turns out my issues with my mom were based on a misunderstanding." As I recounted Mom's revelations and the news of her illness, tears welled up in my eyes again. I had cried all night after Mom went to bed, ridden with guilt and regret. "I can't believe thirteen years ago I left without even saying goodbye to her. I feel terrible."

"Good for both of you. I'm sorry about her cancer." Somehow his words didn't sound genuine. His tone was emotionless.

"Me too." I hesitated. "We just found our way to each other. I hate to think about the cancer."

"Is she getting treatment?" His voice was dry and tired now, as though he was bored with the discussion.

"She doesn't want to spend the rest of her life in hospitals. The doctors said there's nothing anyone can do." I sighed. "I tried to convince her to come and stay with us, but she refused—"

"You what?" Miles cut me off.

"I asked her to come and stay with us. I mean... we have the space, and I could keep an eye on her."

"Why would you do that? You didn't even run it by me."

"She's my mom. I thought you'd understand."

Miles didn't respond.

"Miles, you there?"

"I am. I just don't see why you would do such a thing without consulting me first."

I sat down at the desk, my head reeling. "My mom is sick; I want to be there for her. I didn't think it would be an issue."

"You were wrong. It *is* an issue, damn it. You should have asked me first. You're inviting someone into our home, the place we go to get away from it all."

"Baby, it's not as if she'd live with us forever, just a couple of months."

"This is the same woman you never wanted to see again, remember? The woman who ruined your life? After only a few hours you're not only forgiving her, you're asking her to come and live with us. I don't get it."

I lowered my forehead onto the surface of the desk and closed my eyes. More tears threatened to spill. Why was Miles acting this way? He was the kind of person who would do anything for people in need. He gave away millions to charity. But now that I wanted us to care for my mom, he was reacting so strangely, so unlike himself.

After a moment of silence on both ends of the line, I got it. He didn't want to share me with anyone else. For a year it had been just us. His parents had died in a car accident when he was a child, and my mom had been out of the picture. Miles and I only had each other. Now I was bringing someone else into our lives, someone else important to me.

"Miles, don't worry about it. I don't want to fight. She's not coming anyway. She doesn't want to." I was still a bit upset that he wouldn't make such a sacrifice for my mom, his future mother-in-law. He had lost his mother, but now he would get another through marriage.

He sighed. "Look, baby, I'm sorry. I didn't mean to say those things. I don't know what got into me. It's fine. If you want her to stay with us for a while, it's okay."

"You're so hot and cold. You were so adamant a moment ago that you didn't want her to stay with us. What changed?"

"I don't know. It's been a stressful couple of days. And I have to go on a last-minute trip out of town. I'm on the jet right now."

"Okay." I sucked in a breath. "She... she wants to come to the wedding. Can I invite her?" I had already invited her, but I didn't want Miles to react the way he had a few minutes ago.

"Of course she can come to the wedding. If you've forgiven her, I do too."

That was the man I knew him to be. The caring, loving man I had fallen for.

"By the way, did you sort out what you went there to take care of?"

A chill spread through me. "Not yet. But I will soon. I'm planning on coming back tomorrow." It would be hard leaving Mom in her current state. The thought of leaving her alone again made my stomach hurt. But I would visit Misty Cove as often as I could to see her.

"Good. Have you received any more cards from the stalker?"

The cards. I had forgotten that I didn't receive a card yesterday. My stalker must have lost me. I wasn't being followed in Misty Cove. Maybe they had no connection to my past after all.

"No more cards. I think it was a prank and the person got bored. It could be over." I knew it wasn't over. I felt it. But I couldn't tell Miles that. I had to sort it out before I returned home. Spending my life looking over my shoulder was not an option.

Miles was quiet again. When he spoke, his voice was low and controlled. "I have to go. I'll talk to you later."

When I hung up, I realized that in his rush to get off the phone, he hadn't told me where he was flying to. I shivered. Something about him was off. He wasn't acting like himself.

CHAPTER FIFTEEN

The living room was transformed. Everything was clean and sparkling, no dust or dirt anywhere. Even though my mom still looked sick, she seemed to have a lot more energy and was humming a song when I entered the kitchen. The huge pile of dirty dishes I had seen in the sink yesterday had disappeared.

"Good morning, honey." She kissed my cheek. "I made breakfast, want some?"

"Actually, I was just about to head out. I don't really have time for breakfast."

"Oh, that's a shame, I thought maybe we could eat together." Her face crumpled the way it had when I'd told her about the night that changed my life.

I brushed away our emotional conversation from yesterday and glanced at the kitchen table, recalling all the times we had sat there in silence, day after day, as we ate our food. She hadn't been there for me emotionally, but at least there had always food on the table.

"I'll be back by lunch, and we can eat together then. I really appreciate the effort you put in. Please don't overdo it, though. You need to rest." I hugged her, but not too tight.

"Don't worry, honey. I feel stronger today." She pulled away but held my arms. "I've been thinking about what you said last night. It was a shock to hear, but I blame myself for what happened... what you did. You wouldn't be in danger now if I had been there—"

"Stop beating yourself up. The decisions I made were all mine. You're not to blame."

"But I can't help it." My mom went to fill the kettle. I could see from her trembling shoulders that she was crying. "If only I could do something to make it all go away."

"Mom, really, you have nothing to do with this. It's all me." I reached for an apple, rinsed it, and wiped it with a kitchen towel. "There is something you can do." I leaned against the fridge. "Have you heard anything about my friends? Whatever you know will be a huge help. I need something, anything to go on."

Mom wiped her eyes and turned to me. "Not much. Stacy Prammer only visited once since she went to college, and not long after that her parents divorced. Her mom moved away. Her father died about a year ago."

My heart sank. I wished I could talk to all of

them, to find out if they were also being stalked. It had not even crossed my mind that they might not have returned to Misty Cove after college, as I had done.

"How about Melanie Thompson and Jane Dreer? Are they still in town?" Even though I had not planned on having breakfast, I found myself sinking into a chair and reaching for a slice of fresh bread, tearing it with my fingers. It was warm and spongy. The apple was forgotten for now.

Mom's face softened as she sat down as well.

"Word around is that Jane moved to Europe, but Melanie... She's still in town." Mom lifted a glass of juice to her lips. "Well, life has been unkind to her. Her father made some bad investments and the family lost everything."

"Oh, no. That's so sad." I bit into the bread. It was so good, it distracted me from the bad news I'd just heard. But I had to focus. I put the bread down on an empty plate and directed my full attention to Mom. "How is Melanie now?"

"Well, she's changed. She dropped out of college because there was no money." She sighed. "Now she has a job as an administrative assistant at the Trinity Church of Christ. But she's like a shadow of herself. She doesn't talk much, and doesn't smile. It's been like that for years." Mom took my hand. "I don't think her father's bankruptcy is the only thing to blame.

Maybe that night affected her too."

I dropped my gaze. "I regret what I did. I just didn't know how to get out of the situation."

"You of all people know I'm not a saint; I've made my own mistakes in life. I'm not in a position to judge you or anyone." She glanced at the kitchen clock. "If you want to talk to Melanie, I'm sure she's at the church already. She's usually there by eight."

"Okay. But I think I'll finish breakfast first." I gave her a small smile.

She smiled back, and I saw a flash of the beautiful woman she once was. "Do you think you'll get any more cards… the stalker?"

"I don't know. I hope not. At least I didn't receive anything yesterday. I hope that's the end of it."

Part of me told me to quit the search for answers in Misty Cove, to go on with my life. What if I was searching for answers in the wrong place? What if my stalker really was someone from my present and not my past?

Last night I'd thought of Fred, the lawyer I had dated before Miles. He had been the jealous kind. We dated for over two years, and the breakup was messy. He didn't want to understand that I couldn't be in a relationship where I felt something was missing. He'd accused me of wasting his time.

But Fred couldn't be my stalker. I had woken up in the middle of the night and went online to check out his social media profiles, amazed that he hadn't blocked me. From the look of things, he had moved on completely. He was married and had a baby daughter. Judging from the pictures he posted of his family, he was happy. He didn't seem like somebody who would jeopardize his new life to get back at an ex.

I had been somehow disappointed that it wasn't him. I'd have preferred the stalker to be someone in my current life.

"I hope it's over as well. But please be careful." Mom touched my cheek gently.

I nodded and started to eat, filling myself with enough food to get me through the whole day.

When I walked out the door and down the path, munching on my apple, I couldn't help wondering what had become of my friends. I now knew Melanie's dreams of becoming an actress didn't pan out, but what about the others? Did theirs come true? Were they married with kids? Did the past ever cross their minds?

I moved the apple to my left hand so I could reach into my purse for the car keys. When I looked up again I spotted something on my windscreen, tucked behind the wipers. My heart froze.

It was an envelope.

As I walked to the front of the car, I felt nauseous. My stalker had followed me after all. If somebody was willing to put their life on hold in order to follow me to another town, they had to be dangerous.

I glanced around, hoping I could catch the person watching me. But all I saw were people leaving their homes for work, and uniformed children getting into the school bus. Nothing out of the ordinary.

Where was he? Who was he? My feelings told me it was a man. I couldn't explain it, I just knew.

CHAPTER SIXTEEN

The last time I stepped into the Trinity Church was when my father died, the one time Mom and I had resembled some kind of family, brought together by shared grief. As we listened to the minister, both of us had sat ramrod straight, gazing ahead, so near and yet so far apart. I remembered now that my mom had not cried. At the time I thought she had been consumed with grief, but now I knew she probably couldn't find it in her heart to grieve for the man who had hurt her so deeply.

Neither of my parents had ever really been the religious kind, although Mom had brought me to church occasionally when I was younger. Like with everything else, she stopped out of the blue. I didn't understand why, but I also didn't ask. By then the distance between us was too great to cross.

The Trinity Church was still as beautiful as I remembered, with its vivid stained glass windows and heavy, carved front door. Months after we stopped coming to the church, I would walk by often, contemplating whether I should enter. I used to envy the children playing on the swing in the large yard, or gazing into the koi pond. I hated that I couldn't be part of it. There were times I considered waking up early on Sunday before my parents got up and attending the service alone, but I had been afraid of being turned away. What if the reason we no longer attended church was because we had angered God in some way? What if we had been banished from the church?

I stepped over a puddle of rainwater that reflected the sky, and ran up the stone steps. I pushed my weight against the heavy wooden door. It was a warm morning already, which meant it would be a hot day, but the interior of the church was cool. The sudden change in temperature sent goosebumps scattering across the skin on my arms. As I walked down the aisle, the slapping sound of my leather sandals echoed off the walls. I inhaled the faint scent of burning candles.

Although I needed to go look for the office, I found myself standing in the middle of the aisle instead. In those few seconds, feeling to my heart rate slow down, a sense of calm fell over me. When was the last time I'd prayed? Did God even remember me?

My gaze landed on the large statue of Jesus

that hung from the wall behind the altar, coming to rest at the pulpit.

In my mind's eye I saw the pastor standing up there, offering people hope beyond their pain and troubles. How many people came in here every Sunday carrying their burdens, wishing to leave lighter? And how many left feeling the same way? I was in no position to question God's power, since I didn't even know him. Did he really answer prayers? I decided I had nothing to lose by sending up a little prayer anyway.

"Excuse me, can I help you?" The baritone voice behind me made me jump. I quit praying and spun around. From his robe I could tell instantly that he was the pastor. He was short, with hair so gray it was almost white. Did he have problems too, like the rest of us, or was he immune to suffering?

"No." I nibbled on my bottom lip. "Actually, yes, maybe you can. I'm Chloe Parker. I'm looking for Melanie Thompson. I heard she works here."

"Yes, yes. Melanie is in the office. I'm Pastor Fred Jennings. Please follow me, Ms. Parker."

As I walked behind him, I was glad I didn't recognize him. If he didn't know me, he didn't know about the article I had written, and the chain of events that followed.

A naked lamp hung from the middle of the

ceiling, and yet the wood-paneled corridor was dim and eerie. We turned the corner.

"Here we are." Pastor Fred opened the door. "Melanie, you have a visitor." He stepped aside, allowing me to enter.

In contrast to the corridor we had just left, the office was bright, airy, and spacious. My gaze rested on the woman sitting behind one of the two desks, a huge window behind her, overlooking the sea.

My breath caught as our eyes met and Melanie's eyes flickered. The only familiar thing about her was her unusually gray eyes. The sparkle she'd had in school was nowhere to be seen. Her once shiny hair was limp, her eyes dull and empty, and the bags under her eyes, visible even from the doorway. Where was the girl I had known? The girl everyone had admired? She'd had the best body, the glossiest hair, the longest legs… the best of everything. I had so much wanted to be like her back then. She had been the envy of many girls.

It seemed the tables had turned. I was no longer the frump next to her. My wishes had come true. I *had* become her. My makeup was flawless, my hair shiny, and I was toned and slim.

"This is Ms. Parker. I'll leave you two alone. I have to prepare for Bible study class."

As soon as Pastor Fred left and closed the

door, the shutters went down in Melanie's eyes. My heart sank. I'd be lucky to get any information out of her.

"Hi, Melanie." I swallowed, but my throat remained dry. I felt claustrophobic even inside the large office. I would have loved to turn around and leave, to pretend I'd never seen her... the woman she had become.

"Hi." She looked away. A blush rose up her neck from the collar of her brown flowery blouse. "I'm surprised to see you again." She busied herself arranging the sheets of paper on her desk.

"So am I. I never thought... I didn't think I'd return." Without waiting for an offer, I took a seat on the side of the desk opposite her. What I wanted to discuss was too important to be done standing.

I wished so much I didn't have to dig up the past, to remind her of it. She had gone through a lot already and I felt sorry for her. It wasn't fair what had happened to her family. Tasting luxury and then losing it all was cruel. "How have you been?"

Melanie's eyes met mine again. I saw sadness there, but also annoyance. "Why are you here?" she asked without bothering to answer my question.

"I was in town so I thought I'd come and see you to catch up."

"There's nothing to catch up on. I don't mean to be rude, but I'm busy today." She started punching holes in stacks of papers and putting them into a folder with a label that read "Offering." She slammed it shut and stood, then walked over to one of the filing cabinets, her long, gray skirt brushing her ankles. She pushed the folder inside, next to several others. Then she just stood there, her back turned to me.

"Mel, are you okay?"

"Nothing is okay. But I'm sure you know that already. It's a small town." Her voice was the same, even though she seemed to be stuck in someone else's body.

"Look." I clasped my hands and sighed. "I'm so sorry about everything that happened to your family. My mom mentioned it to me."

She turned around and shrugged. "Things happen."

"If there's anything I can do, please let me know."

"Forget about me; you seem to be doing just fine." Was that criticism in her voice?

"Yes. I'm fine." I swallowed through the dryness inside my throat. "But I never forgot."

"Forgot what?" She returned to the desk and sat.

Was she joking, or did she really not know what I was talking about? I searched her eyes but they were blank. No emotion, like a TV that had been switched off.

"You're kidding, right? Why are you pretending you don't know what happened, what we went through together?"

"Kelly, I've moved on with my life and... so have you. I don't want to talk about the past. Wasn't that what we agreed to that night?" She shook her head. "Why are you here, really? I find it hard to believe you just wanted to say hi. You've been gone for years."

"I'm sorry. I know we agreed not to bring it up again and to go our separate ways. But something is happening in my life and I think... I'm almost positive it's related to what happened."

She raised an eyebrow. "You have problems? Really? Doesn't look like it to me."

"Looks can be deceiving." I leaned back, undid and then redid my ponytail. "I do have a problem. Someone is stalking me. I think that person knows what happened."

"Whatever you're going through, it has nothing to do with me. Maybe you made enemies in your new, glamorous life."

She didn't have to say it. She knew about *Sage*; the whole town probably did. So much for starting a new life as someone else. But I had nothing to apologize for. It infuriated me that Melanie was attacking me. I had not said one unkind word to her. But on some level I did understand her bitterness. I had the kind of life she had wanted for herself. I reminded her of what she had lost.

And the truth was, if it weren't for me, that night would never have happened. At first, Melanie had refused to be involved, but Stacy had talked them all into helping me.

"Please, Mel; I just want to talk. Maybe you know something that can help me figure out who the stalker is."

Melanie laughed and folded her hands in front of her. "Help you?" She scoffed. "Don't you think I've done enough of that? If I could turn back time, you know what I would do? I would refuse to be pulled into your mess. I would have gone to the cops. If I had, I wouldn't be tormented every day by this guilt… this guilt that doesn't belong to me." Her eyes sparkled with fury and I saw she was trembling. "I suggest you go back to where you came from and deal with your own problems. Don't make me a part of it."

"I'm sorry." Tears burned my eyes. "I'm sorry for what I put you through. I just—" I took a deep breath. "If this person is after me because of what happened, you could be in danger too."

"I have work to do. Please leave. There's nothing to talk about."

I pushed myself out of my chair with a sigh. It was impossible to force a grown woman into talking to me. If only the other girls were in town. One of them might have understood that if we were all in danger, the pact of not talking about what happened was null and void.

How would I move on now? Who else could I talk to? "Do you maybe have Jane or Stacy's number? I want to give them a call. I heard they're no longer in town."

"No, I don't." Something flashed in Melanie's eyes, but I had no idea what it meant. "Stacy died two years ago in New Jersey." She stood up then and walked to the door, leaving me reeling from the news she had just thrown at me. She opened the door and waited for me to walk out of her life.

I halted in the doorway. "How did she die? Was she sick? Please tell me more. She was my friend, too." Tears blocked my throat.

"Goodbye, Kelly."

I nodded, but instead of leaving straight away, I dug into my purse and pulled out all the money I had on me—a couple hundred dollars in cash, and my business card. Her eyes widened when I pushed it into her hand.

"If you need any more, give me a call. I'll be glad to help in any way I can."

I didn't wait for her to respond.

***

I sat inside my car, gripping the wheel, still shaken by the tragic news of Stacy's death. Among my group of friends, Stacy had been the nicest of them all. She had treated me with kindness, and looked at me as though she saw me. She'd taken me under her wing. The thought of her being dead not only saddened me, it terrified me. How had she died? Was it from an illness, natural causes? Or had there been foul play?

I leaned my head against the steering wheel, sweat gluing my skin to the leather. Maybe I was driving myself crazy, connecting everything to the past.

I prayed for the torture to end. I couldn't bear it anymore. Being in the dark was killing me, and I was nearing my breaking point.

What did the stalker plan to do with me once the countdown was over? Did he intend to kill me on my wedding day?

CHAPTER SEVENTEEN

A knock on my car window startled me and my forehead hit the horn. The man on the other side of the glass waved excitedly, his huge grin exposing unnaturally white teeth. My heart sank as recognition set in. Great. Larry, my high school crush.

Thirteen years later, I felt nothing for him. I contemplated not opening the window and just pretending he was confusing me with someone else, but then an idea hit me. I rolled down the window and smiled up at him.

A dirty mobile trailer drove by, sending dust particles floating into the air behind him, some of them landing on his now shoulder-length hair.

"I cannot believe it's you, Kelly. How many years has it been?" He still had that perfect smile, but this time it had no effect on me whatsoever.

I forced another smile onto my own face. With so many questions tormenting me, I found it hard to genuinely be happy. Would I ever be happy again after all this was over? Perhaps that was what the stalker wanted—to destroy my happiness until I had none left. "Larry, how great to see you."

"I wasn't sure whether it was you, but I decided to take a chance. It's been so many years since we saw each other. High school feels like a lifetime ago."

How was I ever attracted to him? Looking at him now, he wasn't all that handsome. His eyes were too close to each other, his nose too large, and his once thick hair was already thinning at the top.

"Mind if I come inside for a bit? It would be great to catch up." He pointed to my passenger seat.

I nodded. Larry ran to the other side of the car and slipped inside. He turned to me with that huge grin on his face. He looked like a kid whose Christmas wishes had just come true. "God, Kelly, wow. You look amazing."

"Thank you so much. You look nice too."

He ran a hand through his hair and nodded. "Well, a guy's got to keep the ladies happy. Anyway, I heard you're a magazine publisher now and you go by a different name."

"Yes, my name is Chloe now. I've always liked the name. I thought, why not?" How small was this town, anyway?

"I'm so happy for you. I've been doing well myself. I'm an actor now. I've actually acted in a few movies."

"Really? That's great." It had to be the perfect job for someone who loved being admired for his looks. The problem was, I'd never seen a movie with him in it. "Any movies I'd know of?"

He smacked his forehead. "I should have known you'd ask that. Actually… the truth is, I've been auditioning for a couple of local films, but nothing has happened yet." He looked so embarrassed I almost laughed. "But I've been in a couple of commercials—furniture and soap. He raised an eyebrow. "Maybe if you feature me in your magazine, it could help me get some gigs… What do you say, for old time's sake?"

I hated to tell him the kinds of people we featured were celebrities, people with the kind of fame that sold magazines. "You never know."

He didn't respond. He was too busy eyeing me up and down, from the top of my head, down my breasts and stomach, and then resting his gaze on my lap. I hoped he wasn't thinking about what was underneath my skirt. He was making me so uncomfortable that I shifted, hoping to break his gaze. The guy I had been so crazy about once was finally looking at me as if he wanted me, but I only saw him for the womanizer he was.

In school I had been too desperate to care about the fact that he'd slept with almost every pretty girl in school. I just wanted him to notice me. When he'd asked me to be his prom date, I was so shocked I didn't respond for a full minute. At the time I didn't care that he only wanted to be with me because of the article I had written. Larry had been smart. He loved to be the center of attention. He'd known all eyes would be on me, the fearless girl who went above and beyond to get a story that left everyone in awe. It didn't matter that he was not attracted to me. The spotlight was what he cared about.

Fortunately, or maybe unfortunately, we never made it to the prom together. The sensational article had gotten me banned from going to prom, as well as attending the official graduation ceremony.

"So, how long are you in town for? Maybe we can have a coffee or something."

"I'm not staying long. I'm leaving tomorrow, actually. I won't have time. I have a lot to do in town."

"That's a big shame. It would have been nice to catch up." He cocked his head to the side and gave me a look he probably intended to come across as sexy, but it only made him look desperate. "I've thought about you a lot over the years. I wondered where you had gone off to, whether if you had stayed we might have had something… after our almost prom date. If you ever come to town again, give me a call. I'd really love to have that coffee." He pulled a card from his wallet and handed it to me.

As I reached for the card, I felt a twinge. He was trying so hard. While I was thinking of ways to let him down gently, my gaze landed on the hand holding the card. He wore a wedding band. What an idiot! I met his gaze head on. "You're married? Congratulations."

He gave a nervous laugh and covered his left hand with his right. Did he think if the ring was out of sight it meant the vows didn't exist? My stomach turned, and my heart went out to his poor wife. Thank God I hadn't ended up with him.

"Yeah, I am." He glanced out the window for a moment. When he looked back at me, the confidence in his eyes had returned. "But you know, there's nothing like the kind of bond you form in high school."

"Don't talk like that, Larry. High school bond or not, you're a married man. Be respectful to your wife."

Shame clouded his face. "I guess you're right. I made my bed, now I have to lie in it."

"You got that right." I toyed with a lock of my hair. "Speaking of high school, are you in touch with anyone? I just went to see Melanie."

"I bet you got a shock." He snorted. "Can you believe she's the same girl? She's one big mess now."

"She and her family apparently went through a lot. I think she's doing the best she can."

"But to let herself go like that. She was so hot back then."

Larry's voice made him sound like a man, but beneath it all he was just a teenager, like a boy stuck inside a man's body. "Have you seen Stacy and Jane since they left town?"

"Funny of you to ask that. You guys were friends, weren't you?" He scratched his beard as if he had fleas. "Well, I heard Stacy is dead, but her body was never found. She just disappeared from one day to the next."

"And they just assumed she died?"

"What else could have happened to her? There were all kinds of ridiculous speculations drifting around."

"Melanie told me about Stacy's death. I still can't believe it." Now that I knew her death was not confirmed, I held out hope that maybe she was alive. I'd heard of stories before where people disappeared from their lives with the intention of never being found. Some went as far as faking their own deaths. But what reasons would she have had for doing that? Could she have been running from something... or someone?

"It doesn't matter anymore." Larry cut through my thoughts. "Life goes on. Are you sure you don't want to have a drink with me?"

"Maybe some other time. I have a lot to do before I leave tomorrow. And I have to call my fiancé to let him know what time I'll be arriving in Boca Raton."

"Fiancé." He cleared his throat. "You're getting married?"

"Yes, I am." I lifted my left hand. The sparkle of the diamond still made my heart flutter.

"Who's the lucky man?"

"Miles Durant." I expected he'd know who Miles was.

His jaw dropped. "*The* Miles Durant?"

"You know him?" My heart almost exploded with pride at being the fiancée of one of the most well-known men in America.

"Who doesn't? How could I not? He's one of the greatest successes of our time."

I smiled in response. "Larry, thank you so much for coming to say hello. I really have to get going, though." I paused. "But can I ask you something?"

"Sure, what do you want to know?" The shock of my engagement was still visible on his face.

"Do you know anything else about Stacy?

Whether she was married, what she did for a living? I just… she was my friend. It would be nice to know more."

He rubbed his chin. "She was apparently a wedding dress designer. That's all I know."

"Thanks. It's so sad that she… she died."

"You can say that again." Larry sighed with defeat. "Okay, I'll let you go… future Mrs. Miles Durant."

"It was nice talking to you, Larry. See you again sometime." I bet he wished now that he had given me a real chance in high school.

"Sure thing. See you soon, and congratulations again." He gave me an awkward hug.

After he walked away, it took me a while to start the car and leave. I couldn't stop thinking about Stacy's disappearance. The news had alarm bells ringing inside my head.

CHAPTER EIGHTEEN

A black Rolls-Royce was parked in front of my mom's house. More surprising was the man leaning against it, peering at his phone.

Owen? What in the world was he doing in Misty Cove? And if he was here, where was Miles? Something in the pit of my stomach turned and twisted. My gut told me Miles was with him. Owen would not come by himself, unless of course he had lied, and he was, in fact, my stalker.

Holding my breath, I slowed down behind the car and parked. Owen glanced up from his phone and gave me a fake smile. Of course he wasn't happy to see me. Not after I had accused him of being a stalker. We had not seen each other since the night I tried to go through his phone.

After everything I had found out since coming to Misty Cove, especially Stacy's disappearance, I was pretty sure Owen was innocent. The person who was chasing after me had to be connected to my past. I was sure of it. There was more to what was happening to me, and it wasn't pretty.

I climbed out of the car feeling as if my legs were detached from my body.

"We meet again." Owen said. "What a pretty little town you come from."

"Owen, what are you doing here?" I looked up at the house. "Is Miles with you?"

"Yes, we had a couple of things to talk about. When he mentioned he was taking the jet to come and see you, I thought it would be a good idea to join him... to catch up, you know."

Dread sliced through me. If Miles was in town, it meant he was on the jet when we talked earlier. Misty Cove was the trip he had been talking about. Why hadn't he told me?

To calm myself down, I decided maybe he was in town to surprise me. But what I couldn't understand was, why today? Why didn't he come tomorrow, so he could take me back to Boca Raton with him? Or was he spending the night in Misty Cove? My mind was already bursting with unanswered questions.

"Is everything okay?" I asked Owen. "He didn't mention he was coming."

"Sorry, I can't help you. Miles wouldn't say a word to me about why he dragged us here. But be prepared: He doesn't seem to be in the best of moods." Owen dropped his phone in his pocket. "If you want answers, talk to him. Frankly, I'm not up to discussing anything with you. You seem to enjoy throwing accusations around. Yes, I did a little research on you, but it was due diligence. Calling me a stalker was going too far."

"Can you blame me? You don't like me; that's no secret."

"I'm pretty sure those words never came out of my mouth."

I rubbed my brow, releasing the tension there. "You don't need to put it in words."

"Miles is my friend. I've known him longer than he's known you. I want what's best for him, and I just don't think you two are meant to be together." He shrugged. "But, hell, what do I know? That's for you to decide. But something is bothering Miles. If I didn't know better, I'd think there's a little trouble in paradise."

Although I had wanted to prepare myself before entering the house, I had no choice but to face Miles head-on. I would get no answers from Owen.

I was nervous knowing Miles was here. People liked to talk. What if someone mentioned something to him about my past? My heart thudded when I thought about my mom. Hopefully she hadn't said anything to him. Whatever he was doing Misty Cove, I had to find a way to keep him from coming into contact with anyone else.

Owen took a step toward the gate, and I followed him. As we walked down the path, my stomach churned.

The door opened before we reached it.

Miles burst out, his face a mask of rage. I had never seen him so angry before. My mom was nowhere to be seen.

"Looks like you two need to talk." Owen pushed past him. "I think I'm going to finish those ginger cookies."

"Miles, what are you doing here? Is everything all right?"

Miles shut the door behind him and took my hand, his fingers like a clutch around mine. It was a little painful. What was going on? Why was he so angry? Did he know something?

When we reached the car, he yanked the passenger's door open and slammed it shut again once I was settled inside.

He went to the other side and climbed in beside me. "You tell me, Chloe. I'm here because I want answers. What the fuck is going on?"

My mouth turned dry. "What do you mean? What answers are you looking for?"

He reached into his pocket and pulled out an envelope, the stalker envelope. "I'm talking about this." He waved the envelope between us, holding it as if it were some kind of poisonous thing. "I found it yesterday, in the mailbox. The card, the piece of lace, they're all there."

I reached for the offending envelope and brought it to my chest, wanting to get it as far away from him as possible. The thought of my past and future merging terrified me. No place was safe for me anymore. Not Boca Raton, and definitely not Misty Cove. Here I was, thinking the stalker hadn't sent me a card yesterday.

My blood ran cold. By sending the card to our house, the stalker had made it clear they were trying to reach out to Miles as well, trying to destroy my relationship and everything that meant something to me. How far was this person willing to go? How long until Miles knew what I'd done?

"Did you get another one of those today? Or will I find it sent to our home?"

"I… I…" I stuttered. I knew I should be honest, tell him I found another one on my windshield, but he looked so angry, so different from the man I knew.

"I asked you a question, Chloe." His sharp voice sliced through me. His eyes were frosty.

"No." I dropped my gaze, hoping he didn't already see the truth hidden in my eyes. Lying was the one way for me to save our relationship, even though the guilt made my stomach hurt. "Maybe this is the last card."

"What if it's not? What if your stalker

somehow manages to find out where you are and sends you another one before today is over?" He raked a hand through his hair. "I just don't get it. Why the fuck is this person sending you these cards? What did you do, Chloe? What are you not telling me?"

"Nothing." My eyes welled with tears as I looked down at the card. "Like you said... maybe it's someone who's angry about a story we published in *Sage*." *Please, Miles, don't read too much into this.*

"You know what? The more I think about it, I have a feeling there's more to this than somebody pissed off about an article in *Sage*." His brow knitted. "There's something I don't understand. Why are you here... in Misty Cove? You told me you had something to sort out. What is it?"

The lie came easy. "I just wanted to come and talk to my mom. I've been thinking about inviting her to the wedding for a while. After all these years it was important that we talk in person." I drew in a long breath, held it, then released. "I didn't tell you because I thought you might try to talk me out of it. I told you some bad things about her."

"I have to say I was surprised. You wanted nothing to do with her for a long time."

"I know. It's just that the wedding planners have been asking me for a while if my mom was coming. I couldn't bring myself to say no without at least talking to her." I glanced at the house. "I'm glad I came. I wouldn't have known she was sick."

"Then I'm glad you came too. I thought your visit had something to do with the cards." He shook his head and tucked a strand of hair behind my ear. "When you come back, we have to go to the cops."

Panic tightened my throat. "I don't think we need to get the cops involved."

"What are you so afraid of? This is a crime. Someone is trying to hurt you. Why are you so against going to the police?" He leaned forward with each word until his breath and his suspicions were hitting my face. What did he suspect?

"I'm not." My chest rose and fell with rapid breaths.

"Good. If you get another card, I will personally take you to the cops myself. If you hadn't been so against it, we could have gotten them involved already."

"I didn't want to make it a big deal, since we had suspected it was a simple prank."

"Someone sending you blood is not a damn prank. They could be dangerous." He closed the space between us. His face was so close to mine that his anger burned my skin. Rage exploded in his eyes. "I'm trying to protect you.

If there's anything you're keeping from me, I want to know. I need to know the truth, so I can come up with a plan. What is it, Chloe? What are you hiding? I know there is something going on that you're not telling me. Who do you think this person is? We both know it isn't Owen."

"I'm not hiding anything from you."

He looked at me for a long time, his lips pressed together. "I can't shake the feeling that you're lying to me." He leaned back, a vein throbbing on the side of his neck. "I came here today because I wanted to look you in the eye, to search for the truth. I don't think I'm leaving with it."

I reached out my hand and grasped his. "I'm sorry you feel that way. I don't know what to tell you." I swallowed my tears. "Please, let's forget about this and move on. Let's get excited about our wedding again."

"You understand why it's hard for me to move on, right? You are my fiancée, my future wife. If you're in danger, I want to be involved. It's my job to protect you if I can."

"Yes, I do. And I love you for it. I don't think there's anything more to worry about."

I wished I could close my eyes and open them again to find it had all been a bad dream. That I wasn't in any kind of danger, and there were no shadows chasing me.

Miles reached for me and held me so tight I felt his heart beating against mine. He kissed the top of my head and then moved his lips to mine, brushing them lightly. "I never want anything to happen to you, you hear me? I'm here if you ever need me. You can tell me anything."

"I know." I kissed him, enjoying the comforting feel of his lips. Then I leaned back and met his eyes. Most of the anger had melted away, leaving only traces.

"In any case, when you come back to Boca Raton, I want to hire a bodyguard for you, somebody to watch you to make sure you're safe. Just until we're sure you're not in danger." His expression softened even more. "We could also hire a private detective to look into it. Maybe they'll find something."

"No, that's not necessary." Panic swirled in my stomach. A private detective would be a bad idea. They would dig up my past and find out the truth in no time. Miles would know everything about me. "I want us to move on with our lives."

"Fine, if that's what you want." A shadow passed across his features and he pinched the bridge of his nose.

"Are you okay, baby?"

"I'm exhausted. The merger is proving to be a little more complicated than I anticipated."

He leaned in and kissed my forehead. "I need to get back to the office. Do you want to stay, or are you coming back with us?"

Relief rushed through me. I couldn't let it show. "You're going back already? I thought you were staying a while."

"I wish I could, but I have a lot of meetings to take care of."

"Okay. You two can go ahead. I think I should stay until tomorrow. I want to make sure my mom's okay."

Miles nodded. "Your mom seems nice, by the way." He smiled for the first time since we'd started talking. "I convinced her to come to Boca Raton to see some specialists."

"Thank you. I'm glad you managed to convince her. Maybe a doctor there will be able to help."

"Yeah." He massaged the back of his neck. "I'm sorry about what I said over the phone this morning, how I reacted when you told me you wanted her to come and stay with us. I really don't know what was wrong with me. She's your mom. If you want her to come and stay, I'm fine with it. We have too much space for just the two of us anyway. Whatever you want." The corners of his mouth turned up. "I love you, Chloe. I'll do anything for you. I hope you know that."

I swallowed the lump inside my throat. "I *do*

know that, baby."

"I can't wait to see you tomorrow. We should have dinner or do something nice. I'll leave work early."

I kissed him again. "Sounds great." I held his face between my hands. "I cannot wait to be your wife, Mr. Miles Durant."

"And I cannot wait to be your husband." His eyes crinkled at the corners as he smiled.

I returned the smile. "All right, then. I guess I better go inside. Are you leaving right away?"

"I think it's best. We're going to drop off the car at the rental place and get on the jet straight away. The pilot is waiting. I already said goodbye to your mom. Tell Owen to come out?"

"I will. I was surprised to see him."

"I hope you don't mind that he came with me. He's dealing with some issues in his life and needed a sounding board. And I needed a distraction from worrying about you."

"I feel bad for accusing him of being the stalker."

"Don't worry about it. I understand. You were afraid." He kissed me deeper and pulled back almost suddenly, leaving me breathless. "See you tomorrow, my love."

Five minutes later, Miles and Owen were gone.

CHAPTER NINETEEN

Mom was busy cleaning up the dining table, surrounded by the aroma of ginger. Her frantic movements and the sparkle in her eye told me how excited she had been to meet Miles.

"You look... happy." I threw my purse on the table and sat, physical and mental exhaustion weighing me down.

"Your Miles is a wonderful man. Look what he gave me." My mom stretched out her hand. On her thin, pale wrist was a gold and diamond Rolex. "Isn't it beautiful? I never thought I'd own one in this lifetime."

"Wow—yes, it is. And you deserve it. What did you guys talk about before I came home?"

"They weren't here too long before you arrived." She touched my arm. "Don't worry, I didn't tell him anything."

"Thanks, Mom. And thank you for looking after them. I know you don't have too much energy."

"I've never felt stronger. And he's my future

son-in-law. And Owen, he seems like a lovely young man too."

I looked at my mom as though she had transformed into an alien. How could somebody look at Owen and think he was lovely? But of course he must've turned on the charm. Who was I to burst my mom's bubble?

"Yeah. He and Miles went to college together." I fiddled with my pearl earring. "Mom, there's something I didn't tell you. While Miles and Owen were in college, they developed a popular social app called Torp Mobile. They made a lot of money from it."

"I've heard about it, and I know who he is."

"Miles told you?"

Mom smiled and shook her head, her face flushed.

"What did you do, Mom?"

"When you told me his name, I thought it rang a bell. I knew I had heard it somewhere. So I went online last night and looked him up."

"You did?" I laughed. "And do you approve?"

"How could I not? You're marrying a billionaire. Those girls from high school would die with envy if they knew."

I wanted to tell her it wasn't all about the money, but since she introduced the topic of death, I decided to bring up Stacy. Mom was shocked to hear about her disappearance and alleged death.

"How tragic." She sank into a chair. "It's not right for a person to die so young."

"It took me by surprise as well." I pressed my eyes with the tips of my fingers. "Melanie was the one who told me Stacy was dead, but I bumped into someone else from high school... Larry. He was in the same class as me. He said her body was never found."

"Goodness. That's just horrible." She pressed her hands to her flushed cheeks. "Did you find out anything from Melanie and Larry that can help you?"

"Not really. All I know is that Stacy is dead, and Melanie didn't want to talk to me. She wanted the past to remain in the past."

"What you kids went through *is* a hard thing to live with. Sometimes, pretending something like that never happened is the only way some people cope. That's her way of dealing with it."

"I guess you're right." I removed my shoes and massaged my feet. "I don't want to bring her more pain. I'll have to get the information I need another way."

"I hope this ends soon." Tears flooded Mom's eyes and she wiped them away quickly. "Did you tell Miles what happened? What does he think about it?"

I lowered my head, still ashamed for lying to Miles. "He doesn't know about that night. But he seems suspicious. He came here because he found a card at the house yesterday. I told him I didn't get any more." I pulled one of the newest cards from my purse. "But I did, Mom. I found this on my car, after I left the church. Whoever's doing this knows I'm here."

"Why don't you want him to know? He must love you deeply... for him to come all this way."

"Yes, he does." But another nagging thought entered my mind. Miles had given me the impression that he wasn't only worried about me. It was almost as though he was jealous of my stalker. But I brushed the thought aside. It was ridiculous. "He's a wonderful man, and very kind. But that's the problem. He can be too kind sometimes. If he knew what I did, he—"

"You don't think he will understand?"

"I know he won't understand. If I tell him, everything will change. He will leave me." I buried my head in my hands. "I just wish all this would go away before the wedding."

"So do I." Mom stood. "I'm making lunch— chicken casserole, your favorite. Are you hungry?"

I was grateful she was trying to change the subject, to distract me, but my mind wouldn't stop running, reminding me of the danger I was in. My favorite chicken casserole would not help that. "Thanks, Mom. If you don't mind, let's make it a late lunch. There's some work I need to do first. I'm sure I've got tons of emails waiting. I also want to see if I can find out anything about Stacy online."

"Okay. Come down when you're ready."

"I will." I stood and went up to my old room.

At first I sat on the bed, gazing into space, trying not to think about anything for a few seconds. But the spinning thoughts refused to be stilled.

I gave up attempting to calm down and switched on my laptop. Even though I was on leave, I still intended to fit in some work whenever I could. There were tasks only I took care of even when I was out of the office. I also liked to approve most article ideas my employees came up with—potential stories that could make headlines. But I found it hard to focus on work. All I could think about was my own sordid tale. If the press ever got hold of my story, they would have a field day.

I did some breathing exercises while my computer warmed up, but the knot inside my stomach had no chance of unraveling. I did not even bother checking my emails. I went straight online and typed in "Stacy Prammer + Misty Cove." I got nothing but a few social media accounts belonging to various people who shared the same name.

Next, I typed in "designer Stacy Prammer." Various links started popping up. Most of the information was about her business, but when I went to the company website, it stated the domain did not exist. The business must have dissolved after her death. I clicked on more links and got to see some of the wedding dresses Stacy had designed. They were pretty spectacular. She had always wanted to be a designer, and it hurt to know she was robbed of her dream so early—if she was really dead.

I didn't find anything about her personal life and disappearance—or death—which was what interested me the most.

Finally, I gave up and went to read my emails. Hopefully they would keep me busy until lunch.

As I had suspected, I had hundreds of emails in my inbox, all vying for my attention. Some of them were from Tina, but most had to do with work. There was also one from Kirsten, and then a few others from names I didn't recognize.

I decided to open the personal ones first before getting bogged down by articles and deadlines. I responded to Tina immediately, and confirmed that my mom was coming to the wedding. Then I opened the email from Kirsten. It was a virtual card with a kitten singing, telling me to have a nice day. It managed to bring a tiny smile to my face.

As soon as I closed her email, I noticed another one from an unknown address. I normally didn't click on emails from people I didn't know, but I couldn't help myself. It might contain one of the answers I was looking for.

I regretted it immediately. Nausea slammed into me and I jumped up from my chair. I made it to the bathroom just in time to throw up in the toilet.

After sitting on the bathroom floor for a long time, shaking and feeling cold all over, I stood up again, but had to hold on to any solid surface to help me move myself forward. I dreaded returning to my computer, but I had to see the email again. This time I read the message that had accompanied the single photo. One line.

Is this what you were looking for?

My heart thudded as I scrolled down and looked at the photo again. A woman in a wedding dress, the lace and tulle spread out around her like white foam. It would have been a beautiful wedding photo, if it weren't for the blood that stained the white, or for the smudged makeup, the tangled hair, and the garter belt around her neck. Her dead eyes stared back at me as though they could see me.

For the first time, my stalker was

communicating with me directly. He was everywhere, watching me, taunting me. He could be outside the window right now. I held back a scream as I went to shut the window.

Miles was right: I was in danger. But I couldn't ask anybody for help.

CHAPTER TWENTY

After the proposal, many women dream of the perfect bachelorette party, followed by the perfect wedding and honeymoon. I was no exception.

The night after Miles had asked me to marry him, I'd fallen asleep dreaming of being surrounded by my friends, bubbling with joy as I showed off my ring, reveling in the attention poured upon a bride-to-be. I never thought I'd end up feeling the way I did right now, inside the beautiful Lakeside Terrace Boca Raton, but wishing I could be someplace else.

Everything was gorgeous, just as I would have liked it to be. The round tables were covered with luxury damask covers and adorned with fragile white roses, my favorite flowers. The food and champagne were exquisite. But as breathtaking as everything was, I no longer felt excitement at the thought of my upcoming nuptials. What if the happiest day of my life ended up being my worst nightmare?

What if I ended up dying in my wedding dress just as Stacy had? The thought made my insides quiver.

My eyes darted to the ladies on the dance floor. I had been among them a minute ago—I had to pretend I was having a good time—but I'd just returned to the table.

Dancing with the people I called my friends, most of whom were work colleagues, I couldn't help wondering if one of them was the enemy. At this point, everyone was a suspect in my eyes. Anyone who had ever come into contact with me was my potential stalker or an accomplice. I lived in fear each day, afraid my stalker would show up any moment and catch me by surprise. After seeing the brutal photo of Stacy, I lived in constant fear that I might soon come face-to-face with my enemy.

"Chloe Parker. It's been so long. I haven't seen you at Freyt in a while." Lindsay, someone I knew from the gym, approached my table and pulled out a chair.

"So nice to see you, Lindsay. Thanks for being here." If I had planned my own party, I probably wouldn't have invited her. I felt similarly about a few other people who were present. In the two years we'd known each other, we'd never even shared a drink outside of the gym juice bar. In the past year, since I met Miles, we'd hardly seen each other at all.

This was Kirsten's doing—she confessed she had snuck my phone out of my bag a few weeks ago and invited most of my female contacts to the bachelorette party.

Lindsay reached for a champagne glass that wasn't hers and downed it, then she started fanning her face with her hand, a huge smile pasted on her face. It didn't look real. When I looked at her, all I saw was envy. She wanted what I had, or was about to have, anyway. I kind of felt sorry for her. She'd never been lucky at love. The road she'd traveled was strewn with bad relationships and two broken marriages, and she was only thirty-five.

Lindsay was one of the most gorgeous women I had ever met, with a pixie haircut that complimented her heart-shaped face, and huge green eyes. But she often complained that men were only interested in sleeping with her.

"I wouldn't miss it for the world. With a man like Miles in your life, I knew any party of yours would be spectacular." She flashed another fake smile. "So, how does it feel to be getting married to one of the richest men in the country?"

I shifted in my chair. A few days ago her words would have had a different effect. In just a few days I had transformed into someone else. Back then, I would have beamed at the mere thought of getting married to one of the most eligible bachelors in the country, but right now, Miles's persona and wealth meant nothing to me.

When you're faced with a life-or-death situation, priorities change. Right now I didn't care about the billions attached to Miles's name, the expensive rock on my finger, the wedding everyone was waiting for, the exotic honeymoon he was planning for us. I only wanted him. I wanted to be his wife. I would choose him even without all the money. I wouldn't even mind if we lived in a two- or three-bedroom apartment, as long as I had my man. I wanted freedom from fear, and time to enjoy my life with Miles.

"The money isn't important. I love him. That's all that matters."

"Love is dead, my friend." Lindsay reached for another half-empty glass of champagne and drained it, too. "Trust me. Take the money and run."

"I see." I pushed back my chair and stood, smoothing down my Dolce & Gabbana black-and-red lace cocktail dress. "Please excuse me. I need to discuss something with Kirsten. I'll see you at the gym soon."

"Since I'm not invited to your wedding," she said, raising her voice so she could be heard over the rock 'n' roll song that had just started playing, "I wish you loads of happiness. Maybe you're one of the lucky ones." She raised her glass to me. I nodded and walked away, weaving around some of the guests who were leaving the dance floor to return to their tables for more champagne.

They beamed at me, and some asked to see the ring again. I played along. I did the right things and said the words they wanted to hear, and then I continued looking for Kirsten.

I found her sitting at the bar, talking to one of the bartenders, a man who had doubled as a stripper not long ago. She wore a simple black dress, and her fiery hair was wrapped in a beautiful chignon. Unlike most of the women in the room, she and I weren't skin and bones. Even though we went to the gym and lived healthy lifestyles, we didn't live on salad, water, and wine. Over the years, after trying every diet in the book in an attempt to lose weight, I had found peace with the fact that I was not meant to be stick-thin, and reached a size that I felt was perfect for me. I was not thin, but I was slim and toned, and Miles found that sexy.

I reached the bar and Kirsten got up to kiss me on both cheeks. She gave me a real hug, too. No brief touches or air kisses.

"Hey sweetie, I hope you're having a good time."

"I am. You did an amazing job. I never thought you'd organize something for a hundred guests. You didn't have to put yourself through all the stress."

"Anything for you." We both sat down on the barstools, facing each other. "I never forgot what you did for me, you know. I owe you so much."

Three years ago, Kirsten was stuck in a difficult situation. Her beauty spa, Elements, had been burned to the ground and the insurance company refused to pay out, since one of her employees had been responsible for causing the fire. Kirsten was devastated to lose the business that had been her life. We had been friends for less than a year at the time, but I wouldn't have been able to live with myself if I had done nothing. I gave her the money to rebuild her dream, expecting no repayment.

"I can't believe you still bring that up. You don't owe me anything." Even though I wasn't a billionaire like Miles, *Sage* had given me quite a nice cushion, one I could lean on comfortably for years.

"You have no idea how happy I am to call you my friend."

"I'm the lucky one." I asked the bartender for a glass of water.

Kirsten touched my hand and her face grew serious. "Are you sure you're all right? I kind of got the feeling during dinner that you were distracted. Are the wedding plans getting to you?"

I reached for my water and took a sip while I contemplated what to say. "I'm okay. I've just had so many things going on at work... and my mom being sick, and yes, the wedding has added to the stress as well. It is fun stress, though."

"If I were you, I'd have eloped. What matters most are the vows you'll be making to each other."

"I agree. But we can't let everyone down. Three hundred people have committed to coming. And most of the guests are Miles's business partners."

"Who cares? I bet most people would think it's romantic." She shrugged. "But I guess if you eloped I wouldn't have the chance to strut my stuff down the aisle as your maid of honor."

I smiled, but my mind was far away. What Kirsten had just said gave me an idea. After a few seconds I managed to let go of my thoughts and refocused on our conversation.

"I'm so sorry about your mom, honey. I don't even know what to say."

"Thanks. I still can't believe she only has a couple of months left to live." My heart sank at the thought of Mom all alone in Misty Cove. "Miles and I put off our honeymoon for six months. After the wedding I'm going home to take care of her, since she refuses to come here, except to see a specialist. Miles had to talk her into that one. She insists she wants to die in her own home."

"I think that's a great idea… her coming here, I mean, even for a short while. I can't wait to meet her at the wedding."

I nodded. Kirsten was a great friend. After talking to her for a few more minutes, I could breathe a little easier.

**

On my way home in one of Miles's limousines, my thoughts returned to my conversation with Kirsten. Maybe eloping *was* the solution I needed to get control over my life again. I never wanted anything to come between me and my marriage to Miles. But of course, there were many reasons why we couldn't do it. It wouldn't hurt to bring it up to Miles, though, just to see what he thought.

When I arrived, Miles thanked the driver for bringing me home safely and they said their goodbyes. I was in the bedroom changing when he walked in, a strange expression on his face.

I went to him and kissed him. He kissed me with a hunger I had rarely seen in him before, and then, without even waiting for us to reach the bed, he pushed me hard against the bedroom door, so hard my breath hitched inside my throat. I was turned on, but surprised.

He was like someone else, even being a little

rough. He yanked my bra off and pushed my panties down. Then he turned me around so I was facing the door, my cheek pressed against the wood. Then his finger was inside me, digging deep, building pleasure while he pressed his lips to the back of my neck.

I moaned as desire flooded my every pore. Then, just as I was on the verge of coming, he pulled out. I didn't turn as he unbuckled his belt and unzipped his pants. When he pushed into me, the movement was so intense and rushed, my cheek slid up and down the door. He thickened inside of me. Trying to accommodate him brought both pleasure and pain. He drove into me even harder, groaning with each push, as though he was in pain. Then he let out a tortured, animalistic grunt and exploded inside me. I was about to follow suit, but he slid out at the last second.

"What was that all about?" I walked to the bed and sat down, my cheeks burning. "That was a little unfair, don't you think?" He'd always waited for me to come—always.

He zipped up his pants without meeting my eyes. "Chloe, in case you haven't noticed, the past few days have been hard for me. I hate thinking I'm sharing you with someone else, and I don't know how to stop it. I guess I just needed to let some of the frustration out. I'm sorry, if I was too rough." He came over to the bed and kissed the side of my neck.

"What are you talking about? Who are you sharing me with?"

"Your stalker. He's taking you away from me."

I recalled the look in his eyes when he came to see me in Misty Cove. It confirmed his jealousy. Fucking me like that was his way of trying to claim me, of reminding me that I was his and only his. I blinked. "What stalker? I didn't get any more cards, remember?" Another lie—the cards had not stopped. "No one is stalking me anymore. Let's move on." I placed my hands together, a begging gesture. "Maybe we need to get away from it all. Let's go away somewhere, just for a day or two. Let's do something crazy. I was thinking… maybe we should elope."

"Elope? Chloe, we can't do that. What about all the people we invited to the wedding?"

"We can still have a party, except it will be an after party. I can't wait to be your wife, Miles. The sooner, the better."

"Are you sure about this?"

"Absolutely."

He grinned. "All right, baby. Let's do it. Give me a day or two to plan it."

CHAPTER TWENTY-ONE

"Good morning, Miss Parker. Would you like a glass of champagne as you look around?" The owner of the Lily Boutique gave me one of her brightest smiles while several of her employees paced around the store, trying desperately to catch my eye. As soon as I had entered, and they had recognized me, they stumbled over each other to get to me. The manager, of course, made it clear to them in no words at all that she was in charge of assisting me. She wanted me to spend a lot of money, and she was in luck. I intended to do just that.

"I'd like that, thank you, Liz."

Just because Miles and I would be eloping didn't mean I couldn't look fabulous. As we exchanged vows, I would not be wearing my designer princess gown; I would feel too overdressed with just the two of us. To satisfy the anticipation of all the guests who had been invited to our wedding, I decided I would wear the wedding gown at the after party. For now, I would buy something equally stunning but with less material. Something that would blow Miles away.

I had no idea where we would be eloping, because Miles wanted to take care of all the logistics. I had the feeling it would be on a secluded beach somewhere romantic. It was just what I needed, to get away from it all. Keeping our secret between us—and the pilot who would be flying the jet—would ensure nobody tried to talk us out of our plans. And sharing a secret made me feel closer to Miles. I would be in heaven if it weren't for the stalker ruining everything.

It had taken me a whole thirty minutes this morning before I gathered up the courage to leave the house and come to town without the driver. I had plans I didn't want Miles to know about.

After trying on at least seven dresses and guzzling three glasses of champagne for courage, I opted for a strapless cream and white tea-length dress that felt right. It cost more than I had planned to spend, but it was worth it. To complete the look, and to Liz's delight, I also bought a pair of silk-covered peep-toe heels that cost a fortune.

When I walked out of the boutique, my eyes scanned the street for my dark shadow. I almost ran the short distance from the door of the boutique to the cab that waited for me. I gave the cab driver an address.

The office building I was looking for turned out to be a house on the beach instead—a villa, actually. Feeling as though I were in the wrong place, I rang the bell and a man in his early-fifties opened the door. He was short, pot-bellied, and balding, with a fringe of white hair and a ruddy complexion. He wore slacks with a loose black shirt. When he smiled, a dimple fluttered in his left cheek.

"You must be Miss Parker." He extended a hand and shook mine warmly. "I'm Lester Reading. Please come in."

"Yes, I am. Thank you, Mr. Reading." I entered, still carrying my shopping bag on my arm. I would have left it in the cab since it was waiting for me outside, but I had spent too much money to risk it. What if the cab driver decided to take a peek and then drove off with it?

"Call me Lester. Do you want me to put that somewhere for you while we talk?"

"That's okay. It's not heavy at all."

"Can I get you something to drink?"

"A glass of water would be great." My throat felt dry, and the champagne in my system was making me dizzy.

While he went to a bar in the living room, I stood next to a black grand piano, feeling nervous. I didn't know this man. I'd found his email address online and decided to give him a call. Now here I was, inside a stranger's home. I would have been more comfortable if it had been an office setting. What if he was dangerous? I shook my head. His business had been advertised on a reputable website, one I sometimes used in my job.

I would have hired one of the regular detectives I usually used to investigate a target for an article, but I wanted what I was doing to be as far removed from my current life as possible. And when it came down to it, I needed to know the truth.

"Let's head to the office." Lester handed me the water and walked ahead.

I took the ice-cold water, condensation forming on the glass.

He led me to a large office flooded with natural light thanks to the floor-to-ceiling windows. Late morning sunshine spilled in to every corner. The room was sparsely furnished: a big desk with a large computer on it, a couple of chairs, and a couch covered with all kinds of surveillance equipment. A classic black umbrella stood by the door.

He waved to a chair and went around the desk to take a seat. Leaning forward, he picked up a single die from the table, and turned it around and around in his hand.

I placed my shopping bag at my feet and met his gaze. "Thank you for seeing me on such short notice."

"That's okay. You mentioned you have an assignment for us?" His gray eyes warmed. "This is a family business, but I will be the one handling your case."

"That's great." I didn't care who handled my case, as long as it was handled discreetly. "I have a stalker, and I think he's dangerous."

"Did you alert the cops?"

"I can't do that for reasons I'll tell you about in a bit. I just want to know one thing. All of this will be kept confidential, am I right?"

"Strictly." He made a pyramid with his fingers. "What's said in here stays here. Why don't you tell me how it all started? How long has this person been stalking you?"

I took a long sip of water. "It all started when someone sent me these." I reached into my purse and removed the cards I had gotten so far. "Unfortunately, I destroyed the first two."

Lester opened one of the envelopes, his eyes glued to me. What was he searching for on my face? When he pulled out the card, the lace fell to the desk and he picked it up with a frown.

"Is this what I think it is?"

I nodded. "Yes, it's blood. I tested it, but I'm not sure whether it's human or animal."

Lester observed the lace and card for a while and then put them down. "A person who brings blood into the game is usually someone who would stop at nothing to hurt his victim. You're right, Miss Parker; there's a high possibility you're in danger." He cleared his throat. "I'm going to tell you the same thing I tell every client of mine before getting started on any job. I want to encourage you to go to the cops first, to see if they can help protect you."

"Mr. Reading, my situation is such that I will not be able to go to the cops. Not yet, at least." To make him understand, I told him my story—all of it, the way I had told it to my mom. I started with my past, and ended with my present.

When I was done, Lester picked up a notepad and pen and asked me to repeat the story while he asked me specific questions. When we'd finished, he put down the pen.

"What do you want me to do?" he asked. "How do you think I can help you?"

"Please find out if my suspicions are correct, if the stalker is someone from my childhood. I also need to know what happened to my friend, Stacy Prammer... who killed her. Two days ago, I was sent a photo of a murdered woman in her wedding dress. It was Stacy." I blinked, trying to erase the gruesome details from my mind. "I can forward you the email. Maybe you can try to find out who sent it to me. I want to know if the person who killed her is the one following me."

"That's not a problem. I'll start looking into it today. I'll get back to you as soon as I find any news that could help you."

"I'd appreciate that." I leaned back in my chair. "In two days I'll be going out of town, but I should be back within three days. If you can't reach me by phone, please send me an email or leave a message on my phone."

"I'll do that."

"Can you tell me your rates?" Money wasn't an issue at this point; I was desperate enough to pay him well. I couldn't put a price on peace of mind.

"We take half the money before starting a job, and the rest at completion. Will that be all right?" He pulled a page from his notepad and jotted down a figure. It was huge, but I didn't flinch. First, it gave me a kind of confidence in his services. Plus, the amount was justified, as he would need to travel to Misty Cove and New Jersey.

"That's fine. I'll wire you the money by the end of the day." I stood up and picked up my shopping. "Thank you for your help, Lester. I look forward to hearing from you."

The next stop I made was the Coffee Star

Café, where I was meeting Kirsten for a drink.

It would be hard not to tell her about the elopement, even if it was her idea in the first place. But I had to keep it a secret. If one person knew, they might tell someone else. The last thing we wanted was for it to end up in the papers. Good news, just like bad news, was hard to keep hidden. Even Miles agreed not to say a thing to Owen, whom he told pretty much everything.

Kirsten was already waiting when the taxi dropped me off at the café. She eyed the taxi as it pulled away.

"What happened to your car?"

"It's at the mechanic. I thought it would be nice to use a cab again; reminds me of college when my crappy car used to let me down."

"You should have used a bike. I loved mine so much in college. Come on, let's go in." Kirsten hooked her hand in the crook of my arm and led us inside.

The café was populated with people who seemed to have all the time in the world. Most of them were reading newspapers, or gazing down at phones as they drank their coffees and ate muffins or cake. The smell of ground coffee beans was heavenly.

Kirsten and I had discovered the little café on Canyon Street two months ago and we found every excuse to meet here. Since I had so many morning meetings, we often planned to meet at lunch. They served delicious sandwiches. Now that I had time off, I was able to do something out of my regular schedule.

I loved the slow-paced atmosphere at Coffee Star. We could sit and chat for a while without feeling as though we were being rushed to drink our coffee and leave. We sat at our usual booth in the back and ordered vanilla lattes, then talked about Kirsten's business until they arrived.

"Thanks again for the party. It meant so much to me." I sipped my latte. "By the way, why did you choose to have it on a Wednesday? I was surprised so many people showed up in the middle of the week."

"Many of your friends had plans for the weekend. So I thought, why not do it during the week? I figured only people who really cared would come."

"Good point." I propped my chin on my hand. "Enough about me and my wedding. How are *you*? How are things with Patrick? "

"Okay, I guess, when he's in town. But I have to admit the distance is getting to me."

Kirsten and Patrick met five months ago online. He was a doctor in Washington, and she liked him so much she decided to give a long-distance relationship a shot.

"If distance wasn't an issue, would you think

he's the one?"

She shrugged. "I thought so, but now I'm not sure. He asked me something, but I still haven't given him an answer."

"What happened? What did he ask you?"

"He suggested we also see other people."

"Like an open relationship? You're kidding me." I pushed the latte aside. For some reason, it didn't taste as good as it normally did.

"I'm serious. I don't even know why I didn't just tell him straight up that I had a problem with it. I don't really want to see other people."

"Wait, you were considering it?" That in itself was shocking to me.

"I don't know." Kirsten gave me a look that reminded me of a puppy that wanted to be cuddled. "Maybe."

"You know what that would mean, right? You'd be sharing him with other women. He'd be having sex with them, and you."

"I know. It hit me hard last night and I sent him an email. I told him I can't do it."

"What did he say?" I looked past Kirsten's shoulder and for a moment I froze—a familiar-looking man entered the café and our eyes met. He was tall, with dark looks, and wore a black three-piece suit. Our gazes held for a heartbeat, and then he went to an empty table. I was so paranoid these days, fearing everyone was out to get me.

"He hasn't responded yet. It sucks. For the first time in my life I really like someone... I feel like I'm in love. And now this."

"I'm so sorry, sweetie." I placed a hand on hers. "You *will* meet someone worthy of you. He's out there. If it's not Patrick, it will be someone even better."

"You're so right." Kirsten sat up straight. "If Patrick insists on having an open relationship, I'll break up with him. I deserve better. And for now I can celebrate true love... yours. I cannot wait for your wedding. You and Miles make such an amazing couple."

CHAPTER TWENTY-TWO

When I got home, Owen's car was parked in the driveway, next to Miles's Mercedes. My heart sank as I walked into the house.

Mary met me at the door and told me Mr. Firmin was inside. Not that I needed to be told.

"Thanks, Mary." I sighed and went to find him.

I found Owen in the dining room, having a brunch of eggs, bacon, sausages—and pizza. A beaten-up brown leather jacket hung from the back of one of the dining chairs.

"Good afternoon, Chloe. How are you today?"

"I'm fine." I made it clear with my tone that I wasn't pleased to see him. Asking our cook to make him breakfast was going too far. It would be a different story if we had all been home, having breakfast together. "I see you're enjoying your food."

"Your chef prepares the best food. I might just steal him for myself." He waved me over.

"Come and eat with me. I can't finish all this on my own."

Was he really inviting me to my own table? "No, I'm fine, thanks. I have a few things I need to do."

Owen lowered his fork. "Watching your weight before the wedding, are you? You don't need it."

"Did you just give me a compliment?" I found myself smiling. "What are you doing here, anyway? Miles is in meetings all day."

"I didn't come to see Miles. I wanted to talk to you."

I raised an eyebrow. It felt like the two of us had never had a proper conversation before. "You want to talk about… what exactly?"

"I'm being a good best man. I thought since you're marrying my best friend, it's my duty to exchange a few kind words."

"Are you sure you know the meaning of kindness?" I met his deep blue gaze. "I don't even think kind words are in your vocabulary."

"Okay. I'm trying to reach out here. I'm trying to create a relationship with you. Why do you have to fight it?"

"Fine, let's talk. I'll go up and change. I'll be down in a bit. Enjoy your food."

I shook my head as I left the dining room and went upstairs to the bedroom, changing into jeans and a t-shirt, annoyed that Owen had showed up unannounced. Wasn't it a little too late for him to start acting as though he liked me? But he was right. He was my future husband's best friend, and he would be around for a long time. I had to make an effort to be at least cordial. And I did owe him an olive branch after accusing him of being my stalker.

I hoped he was innocent. Being stuck in the house with a man who wanted to hurt me was not my idea of fun. But then again, Mary and Cory—the chef—were in the house as well. Owen couldn't do anything to me.

By the time I came downstairs, he was in one of the living rooms, sitting properly on the couch instead of sprawling across it. The TV was off as well. That was a first.

"I'm glad you came down. I thought you'd changed your mind about having a chat with me and had climbed out of a window."

"What kind of host would that make me?" I considered sitting on the couch furthest from him, but it would be rude. So I sat down on the same couch, but at a safe distance. Thank God it was big enough for at least five people. I twisted my body to face him. "So what do you want to talk about, Owen?"

"Chloe, I know we didn't start things off on the right foot. In the beginning, when Miles introduced you to me, I just didn't trust you. I have an excuse for that. Most of the women

Miles dated in the past weren't trustworthy. They were more interested in his money."

"You thought I was the same. How can you judge a person before even getting to know them? I have my own money, I don't need Miles's."

"I was being careful. Miles is often distracted with work. When it comes to his personal relationships, he's never taken the time to do proper due diligence."

"So you were just looking out for him, is that it?"

"That's what a good friend does. And I consider myself to be one." He gave me a lopsided smile. "What I'm trying to say is: I was wrong about you. You really do love him. And he seems to feel the same way. "

"You're only realizing that a year later?"

"I'm sorry it took me a little while. I'm slow with some things."

"Owen, you disliked me so much that the first day we met, you left before the food arrived."

"There's no excuse for what I did. I was a total jerk." He shrugged. "I'm trying to make up for that. From now on, I want us to have a normal relationship. If you're open to it."

I laughed, and I wasn't being sarcastic this time. I never thought Owen would ever make me laugh. The only thing he'd managed to do before was get on my nerves.

"I'd like that, Owen. I appreciate that you're part of Miles's life and that you're looking out for him. I assure you I love him for the man he is and nothing else."

"You know what's funny? Miles was the one who looked out for me first, back in college."

"Really? How?"

"Well, I used to be that guy... the one people referred to as a geek, the one who was picked on in high school and even college. When Miles came to UF, he changed that in a punch... literally."

"Get out of here. You, a geek?" As if for the first time, I noticed just how handsome Owen was. His looks were clearer now that his attitude didn't stand in the way. His eyes were piercing, and without the beard, I could observe his strong jaw. He even had a nice smile. If I had to be honest, he was even more handsome than Miles.

"You wouldn't think it, looking at me now. It took a lot of work and exercise to get me here, believe me." He laughed out loud and pointed two thumbs at himself. "But before *this* Owen, there was a little boy and then a teenager who everybody loved to walk all over."

"I'm so sorry to hear that." My heart clenched.

"Well, as you know, Miles is a hero. He hates

anybody being treated badly. The first week he arrived, I got in a fight... a one-sided fight, actually, since the punches I threw didn't even graze the other guy. I was on the ground bleeding when Miles showed up and beat the crap out of the guy."

"Miles, in a fight?" I laughed out loud. "I can't even imagine that."

"You better believe it. He had one hell of a punch. From the moment he threw that punch and knocked over the son of a bitch, people found respect for him, and me. Even though he never fought again, he became a force to be reckoned with. Let's just say he gained his respect from the get-go. I like to think I helped him get it."

"So you two became good friends?"

"Yeah. The next year we rented an apartment together and became roommates as well. We had so many good times. Developing the app just brought us closer. He's like a brother to me."

"It must be hard now that you're no longer working for the company."

"It is, but it's my own damn fault. The money and the alcohol went to my head. But no more alcohol for me. I'm done with that shit."

"Do you want to try and go back? To the company, I mean? I'm sure Miles would rehire you if you showed interest."

"Thing is, I'm kind of enjoying my freedom right now. At the time I was kicked out of Torp, I had a lot of shit going on in my life... personal problems, you know. I still do."

"Does it have anything to do with a woman? You've never introduced us to anyone. Are you seeing someone? I'd love to meet her."

"At the moment, the girls I'm seeing are not worthy of introducing. They don't stay long enough in my life."

"Well, once you meet the one, invite her over here for dinner." I ran my palms over my thighs. "Owen, you're not the only one who should be apologizing today. I'm also to blame for our relationship. I knew from the start that you didn't like me, so I went on the defensive. I didn't try very hard to be friends."

"Fuck yesterday. We have the future to look forward to."

"I agree."

He looked at me for a long time, as though he wanted to ask me something uncomfortable. He cleared his throat, then asked, "did you find out who was sending you the cards, the person you thought was me?"

"If you don't mind, I'd rather not talk about that. We're having a nice time. Let's not spoil it."

"Come on, tell me. Maybe I can help in some way."

"I appreciate that, but don't worry about it. I'll be fine. I am fine."

"You should get someone to watch you... a bodyguard. We wouldn't want you to get hurt. I can arrange for one if you like."

"Miles hired someone. He was supposed to show up this morning but he called in sick. So there's someone else coming tomorrow." I was glad the bodyguard didn't come today. I wouldn't have wanted him to know I met with a private detective.

"That's good." Owen stood and pushed his hands into his pockets. "By the way, I needed something from Miles's office... for the wedding. Do you know where the key is?"

"Sure, I'll go and get it for you." Miles always kept his office locked, probably so our staff did not go in there. I knew where a key was, though I'd never felt the urge to go into his personal space.

"Thanks, Chloe."

"I'll be right back." I left the living room and went to the bedroom. I'd seen Miles put the key inside one of his leather watch boxes in his walk-in closet before we went to bed. I found it and took it to Owen, who was already waiting outside the office door. I waited outside for him to come out of the office, and when he did, his face was pale.

"Are you okay? You look unwell." I touched

his arm.

Owen pressed the folder he was carrying to his chest and gave me the key. "I'm fine. I've got to go."

He left me standing there, utterly confused. What had he seen to upset him like that? I paced around in front of the office for a while and then went inside to see if I could find something. After five minutes of opening drawers and going through shelves, I found nothing out of the ordinary. I left, locking the door behind me.

CHAPTER TWENTY-THREE

Even though Dr. Monroe was often booked for months in advance, Miles had managed to get an appointment with him. He specialized in my mom's type of brain cancer.

She flew into town yesterday evening. It had been just a few days since I'd seen her, and she looked different from the gaunt woman I had met when I got to Misty Cove. Though she was still weak, and I could see she was trying her best to hide her pain, her cheeks seemed to have filled out slightly, and there was a bit of color in them.

As we left the clinic and walked to my car, I couldn't help glancing over my shoulder. I did it often these days, even though I knew my new bodyguard was always close and watching. I was a mess inside, but I did my best to be present while spending time with my mom. I didn't want to waste a moment we spent together. To relieve her of my worries, I told her the same lie I told Miles, that the cards had stopped coming.

And I never mentioned the email I received.

I was all alone now—alone with my fears and my regrets, unable to share them with anyone but the detective.

"Thank you, sweetheart... for everything."

"You have nothing to thank me for, Mom."

"I do. I'm grateful that you came back home, that you found me. I never..." Her voice broke. "I would never have imagined that I'd see you again. I can't believe you're back in my life."

"All water under the bridge." I put on my sunglasses and started the car. "You're here now; we have now. Nothing else matters."

My mom planted a kiss on my cheek. "You're right. Let's make the most of now."

I also hadn't told her about our plans to elope. I hated to see the disappointment in her eyes when she discovered she would not be there when her only daughter exchanged vows with the man she loved. Even though there would be a celebration, the ceremony was what held the most weight, and only Miles and I would be a part of it. All she knew was that Miles and I would be flying out of town in the morning to attend a fundraising event.

I pushed my thoughts of guilt aside and drove to Noir, the restaurant where I had booked us a table for lunch. For the second time since arriving in Boca Raton, my mom was rendered speechless by luxury. It took her a while before she had the courage to touch the food on her plate. She kept repeating that it was a sin to eat something that looked like a work of art. Good thing she didn't know the cost. I wouldn't have been surprised if she sent the food back.

But the pleasure on her face was priceless as she tasted her Creole shrimp and lobster bisque. Watching her warmed my heart and broke it all at once. Knowing I had given her even a moment of joy meant the world to me, but on the other hand, it hurt to think these little moments were all we had left together. I wouldn't be able to do this for her a few months from now.

Despite my fears of losing her so soon, I still held on to the hope that all the tests Dr. Monroe was running would reveal that something could be done. If they couldn't eliminate the cancer, maybe they would be able to add a few more months to her life. The results would be in by the time we returned from our quick wedding, so I could be by her side when she got the news. I hoped it wouldn't be just a confirmation of her death sentence.

I was making the most of our limited time. Mom planned to return to Misty Cove by the end of the day today. I had tried to convince her to spend another night and fly back in the morning, but she wouldn't have it.

"I don't want to be the kind of mom who overstays her welcome. You have a good man; I don't want to mess that up for you."

When dessert arrived, I tried to change her mind again, but she refused to budge.

She dipped her spoon into her chocolate pudding. "We don't have to be living together to be close. Just being able to talk to you on the phone is amazing to me. You've already done enough, honey. For that I'll always be grateful."

"Mom, you're really not intruding. I want to take care of you, and Miles is okay with it."

"Don't you see it? You *are* taking care of me."

"I wish I could do more." My gaze drifted to a man at another table. Maybe it was just my imagination, but I thought he resembled the man I had seen at Coffee Star. My heart tumbled inside my chest, and sweat popped up on my forehead. I had to pull myself together. Mom couldn't see the fear on my face. No way would I spoil the day for her. Luckily, she was too engrossed in her pudding to notice the panic on my face.

I tore my gaze away from the man, told myself it was nothing. He was just another guest. Just because he had the same dark hair and build didn't mean he was the same man from Coffee Star. This man was eating with his female companion and didn't even look at me as he conversed with her.

I glanced at my phone, in case I'd somehow missed a call from Lester. The wait was killing me. I constantly checked my email, but there was nothing useful from him yet. The only email I had received from him was from last night. He was flying to New Jersey to see if he could find out anything more about Stacy's death. He would get in touch as soon as he got back, but he wasn't sure when that would be.

"Guess what we'll be doing after we leave here? I'm taking you shopping."

"Why would you do that? I don't want you spending any more money on me. I'm sure the medical fees will be huge."

"You don't have to worry about the money, Mom." I leaned forward and whispered, "Miles and I have enough."

"Keep what you have for your children or give it to charity. It will be wasted on me."

"Just because they say you only have a couple of months doesn't mean you can't be spoiled. I think you should live every day to the fullest. What do you have to lose? And maybe Dr. Monroe will be able to do something for you."

"I'm afraid of getting my hopes up."

"You know we have to buy something for the wedding. You are the mother of the bride. You can't say no to being spoiled."

I studied my mom's features. She had worn a bit of makeup, and she looked nice. But I wanted her to see herself the way she used to be in the past, even for a day. I would make sure she got the most beautiful dress for the after party, and my makeup artist was also on standby to do her makeup the day of. I hired a photographer just for her, and he would be doing a photo shoot before we left for the reception that morning. I wanted to freeze all the memories of her being happy and beautiful, before pain and death erased it all.

"Okay." She smiled. "I guess it would be lovely to look nice for your wedding."

"Not nice… stunning."

After lunch we went to Caroline's Boutique, which sold designer evening gowns for women over fifty. It was fun watching my mom dress up and admire herself in the full-length mirrors. Even though she had not wanted to come shopping initially, she was glowing. I liked distracting her from her illness. She settled for a lavender chiffon evening gown that flowed to her ankles. It fit her to perfection. A bolero jacket, a matching handbag, and velvet pumps completed the look.

When we left the boutique, she kept glancing at the back seat, as though worried her dress would somehow disappear.

We arrived home just as the sun was setting,

tailed by the bodyguard's car. The shopping had taken longer than we anticipated. After the boutique, we had gone on to buy her some jewelry.

The chef and housekeeper had both left at Miles's instructions, and he was in the dining room, laying the table.

"You two had a long day. I hope you had a nice time." He returned to the table to fold the cloth napkins.

"It was so wonderful, Miles. We also had lunch at Noir," I told him.

Mom settled into one of the dining chairs with a sigh. She was exhausted from all the shopping. On the way home, I managed to convince her to stay the night. I'd already called Miles to tell him he didn't need to get the jet ready for her flight back to Misty Cove.

"What did Dr. Monroe say?"

"Not much. We'll know more when the results come back."

"Let's hope for the best. For now, go ahead and freshen up. I've made dinner."

"When did you get the time to cook?" Mom asked him. "Kelly... Chloe mentioned you had so many meetings today."

"Yes," I added. "I thought you'd have a lot to do before..." I caught myself before I gave away our secret. "Well, I mean, you've been so busy lately."

"Work can wait. I wanted to treat you." He turned to my mom. "Evelyn, I'm glad you're spending the night."

"Thank you, Miles." Mom smiled up at him with open adoration. "My husband used to be a great cook."

My heart clenched as her words brought to life memories of my father, the man who destroyed her, the man responsible for us losing so much time in each other's lives. He *had* enjoyed cooking, and he'd always helped Mom with the washing up afterward, kissing her in-between. How could a love like that just die? How could he have turned to another woman? He had given us so much and then taken it all away. I would never have imagined he was the kind of man who was capable of causing my mom, or any woman, such pain. But it seemed life was full of nasty surprises.

Dinner was pork chops, potatoes, salad, and vanilla cake. It was delicious as usual, and Mom wouldn't stop complimenting Miles on his cooking skills.

At the start of dinner, Miles kept nodding and smiling, acknowledging Mom's compliments. And then, as I watched his face, he didn't seem to be present anymore. At first I thought maybe he was bored, but he kept glancing at his phone. Maybe he was stressed about work. After a while, in the middle of the dessert, he tossed his napkin on the table. He left the dining room without even excusing himself.

"Did I say something wrong?" Mom gave me a worried look. "Should I go and apologize?"

"You didn't say or do anything wrong, Mom. I think… it's just something to do with work. I'll go make sure he's okay."

As I stood up, my mind raced. It wasn't polite of him to get up and leave the dinner he had cooked for us without saying a word.

We had to talk through whatever was bothering him. We were getting married tomorrow. I didn't want him to be miserable on our wedding day.

I found him in our bedroom with his head in his hands. He looked up when I entered. His eyes were empty, giving nothing away.

"What happened back there? Are you okay? You left the table so suddenly. My mom thinks she said something to upset you."

He rose from the bed and walked to the window. "I'm just stressed, that's all."

"Stressed about work, or about us eloping?"

He turned around to face me. "It's work. More issues with the merger."

Despite his work problems, he had taken the time to cook dinner for us, and even pretended to be okay during the first half of it. "I'm so sorry to hear that." I went to him and touched his shoulder, but he shrugged me off.

"Miles?" My voice trembled.

"I'm sorry." He rolled his shoulders. "I didn't mean to do that. I have this massive headache."

"It's okay. Take a painkiller and get some rest." I lowered my voice. "Are you sure you still want to elope tomorrow? We can cancel, and you can take care of business."

"No, I want to marry you. You are my priority. Everything else can wait."

His words made me feel warm inside, but worry still clouded my mind. "Think about it tonight. If you change your mind, I'll be okay with it."

"That's not going to happen." He pulled me close. "I've been waiting a lifetime for you. I will never change my mind about marrying you. I don't know how to postpone the happiest day of my life."

Feeling somewhat better, I went back to finish dinner with Mom while Miles got ready for bed. I assured her he was just stressed about work and she had nothing to worry about.

Afterward, we watched a movie together in the small in-house cinema Miles and I hardly used, and talked in hushed voices. We talked about the present, avoiding the past and the future.

It was nice to enjoy each other's company,

enjoying the moments as they came.

CHAPTER TWENTY-FOUR

Miles was out of bed before me, at 5 a.m., and instructed Ed to drive Mom to the airport. When Miles returned to the bedroom, he was on the phone, and stayed on it for an hour. He wasn't the same man who had left the dining table last night. He was less stressed, and even looked excited and happy. It was infectious.

I didn't get much sleep last night, wondering whether he would change his mind about eloping by morning. He didn't. He woke me up with a kiss and wished me a happy wedding day.

But at the back of my mind, I wondered whether his bad mood last night had something to do with Owen. They used to talk a lot on the phone, and he was constantly at our house. Miles hadn't even mentioned his name lately. And when I brought him up, Miles changed the subject.

What had Owen seen in Miles's office that had caused him to storm out the way he had when he came over to see me?

No. All of that was forgotten for now. Today

was our wedding day, and I refused to worry about anything. *Please don't let the stalker follow me to our wedding.* It would terrify me to find cards at an undisclosed location. Since Miles offered to plan everything, I told him not to tell me, that I wanted to be surprised. In truth, I didn't want the stalker to catch on, in case he was listening to our conversations without our knowledge. After all, he had found out I was looking into Stacy's death and sent me that photo.

My hope was that by the time he figured out we had flown out of town, he would not be able to get hold of transportation to follow us, not fast enough. And he would not know where we were headed. It was easy for him to follow me by car, but he might not even have access to a private jet to chase us across the sky. Hopefully, for the next couple of days, I would be able to let go and enjoy myself, without the fear of being followed. Perhaps while I was away, I would hear from the detective and decide what my next course of action would be.

Before we left, I dressed in a beautiful Dolce & Gabbana black-and-white lace cocktail dress. The butterflies in my stomach, brought to life by the excitement of getting married to Miles, fluttered uncontrollably. But they fluttered around the knot in the pit of my stomach that I tried desperately to ignore. I knew it would not go away until I found out who was following me. I had to learn to live with it for now.

By 8a.m., Miles and I were ready to leave.

Miles called the housekeeper and chef and told them they didn't need to come to the house for the next two days, as we would be out of town. He did not specify where we were going, which was just perfect.

We took one of Miles's less-used cars, a BMW convertible, and drove ahead with the bodyguard following us. He would accompany us until the airfield, and then he, too, would be dismissed until our return. I was so glad Miles had not mentioned the cards again since he'd hired the bodyguard, and I'd assured him I had not received any more. Not discussing it meant not lying to him yet again. But he did insist that the guard watch over me for a couple of weeks anyway. Once we got to wherever we were going, he said he would be hiring another guard on location, just to be on the safe side. I didn't object. I felt safer with the guard around, as I could not rely on myself for protection. It only got complicated when I had to do things Miles knew nothing about, like meeting Lester.

On the way to the airfield, where the jet was parked, Miles confided in me that he would be the one flying us. My eyes widened. I had no idea he even knew how to fly a plane.

"I'm full of surprises, my darling." He

wrapped an arm around my shoulders and I leaned into him, inhaling his intoxicating cologne.

"I guess you are. When did you learn to fly?"

"Soon after I left college. Owen and I took some courses together. Flying was one of them."

"That sounds like fun."

"It was. Flying is so liberating. I like the power it gives me."

"I'm sure it is, though I don't think it's something I would want to do. I'd be too frightened."

Ten minutes later, we arrived at the airfield, and Miles helped me into the aircraft. Although I had flown in it a couple of times, mostly on those days when he decided he wanted us to have dinner or lunch in another state, it still took my breath away. It had all the luxuries imaginable: polished wood, soft leather, glass cabinets, and a fully equipped fridge.

When we rose into the air, I exhaled, the tension dissolving from my body. As I looked outside the window, watching the houses and buildings shrink below, a warm, fuzzy feeling spread through my chest. I was flying away from my troubles. Up here, next to my future husband, I was untouchable. I had no idea how long the feeling would last, but I would enjoy it as long as I could. No use worrying about the next hour when I could enjoy five minutes of freedom and safety.

Miles looked sexy in his flying gear. From time to time, he turned to glance at me, a curious expression on his face.

"I'm not going anywhere. You know that, right?" I smiled.

In my life, I had made a lot of decisions, some of them wrong. Miles was the best decision I'd ever made. We complemented each other in ways I could never have imagined. And even though we had a strong bond, we were still individuals. In the next few hours, I would be Mrs. Durant, one more step away from the girl I used to be.

I was well aware I would not be able to keep my secrets from Miles for much longer. He would be my husband, and if the stalker persisted, he would eventually find out. The worst thing would be for him to find out before I had the chance to explain, to defend myself. Maybe he would understand, and maybe he would find a way to protect me without going to the cops. Doing it all alone was just plain exhausting, and so was trying to keep a secret from the man I loved. I hoped I would still be allowed to call him my husband after he found out the truth.

After about twenty minutes of watching the clouds drift by, the exhaustion of the past few days, of the sleepless nights and constant looking over my shoulder, overtook me. This time, I was able to relax enough to fall asleep. Miles reached for my hand and kissed it.

"Get some rest. You'll not be getting much of it later." He gave me a mischievous smile.

I kissed him on the cheek and left the cockpit, heading for the comfortable bed in the back.

Miles woke me after about an hour so I could get something to eat. I was still drowsy. I ate half a sandwich and went back to bed.

This time, before falling asleep, I downed a sleeping pill, ensuring my sleep would be undisturbed. Miles had mentioned we had a long way to go, although he still didn't tell me where our destination would be.

I didn't care where we were headed, as long as I ended up with him.

CHAPTER TWENTY-FIVE

"Wake up, my sunshine." Miles woke me with a kiss.

I opened my eyes, stretching and looking out the window at the same time, feeling as though I had been sleeping for four days.

"You were really out. Did you sleep well?" He lifted the blanket from me and folded it carefully, placing it at my feet. "You looked so comfortable, I didn't want to wake you."

"I think you did the right thing. If you had tried to wake me, I think I would've snapped at you. Not a great way to start our marriage. How long have I been sleeping?"

"About three hours." I gazed out the small window, trying to make out our surroundings. "Are we here?" My eyes cleared and I noticed the ocean stretching to the horizon. "Where exactly is *here*?"

"Once we step off this jet, *here* will be the *Vendetta*, my private yacht. Isn't it liberating not knowing where you are? Just forget about everything, forget about time, forget about cities and countries. Let's have some fun. Can you do that?"

"Oh yes, I can do that. I had no idea you owned a yacht, though. Since when?" It wasn't as if he couldn't afford one, but he had never mentioned it to me before. In a few hours, I had found out he could fly a plane, and now he had a yacht he'd never told me about. At first, my instinct was to be annoyed at him for keeping secrets, but then I remembered I was keeping the biggest one of them all.

"I thought you wanted to be surprised. I figured we've spent enough days in hotels. I wanted to do something different for our wedding."

"You're right." I kissed him. "You're so romantic." I didn't mention that a private yacht was also the best place for me to hide.

As we got off the jet, fresh, salty air wrapped itself around me, welcoming me to an unknown place. The sky was dimming, and the colors painted across it were vibrant and breathtaking. I could have stood there for hours, in the middle of the patch of airfield, allowing the beauty of nature to captivate me.

I had taken off my shoes, because as soon as we left the jet, we walked onto a long, sandy beach. The sand was warm and soft beneath my feet. Apart from palm trees and seagulls, the beach was deserted, and I almost wondered if it also belonged to Miles.

He carried our luggage while I held my purse. I walked behind him. It felt great not having to look over my shoulder.

I looked up, and my gaze landed on a magnificent, sparkling white yacht. It was the most beautiful boat I had ever seen, and on the side the name *Vendetta* was printed in gold and black letters. I was taken aback by just how big it was.

At the dock, Miles placed the bags at his feet. He wrapped an arm around my waist, his fingers grazing the side of my stomach. "This is it. Isn't it beautiful?"

"I don't know if beautiful is the right word. It's gorgeous, Miles." I couldn't take my eyes off the yacht. "Why did you call it the *Vendetta*?"

He seemed to stiffen a little, and I heard a tiny intake of breath.

"I couldn't decide on a name... *Vendetta* sounds powerful. I always liked that word."

"Well, name aside, the *Vendetta* is out of this world."

"Wait until you see the inside." He took my hand and led me up the stairs of the dock. "Let's go."

I was too excited to walk slowly to the yacht. Giggling like a child, I let go of his hand and raced to it, arriving there before he did, huge grins on both of our faces.

He led us inside, and I was transfixed. I had seen beauty, but this was something else. The luxury was palpable.

The interior design was similar to that of his private jet. As he showed me around, I was tongue-tied. I had been dating a billionaire for a year, so it was surprising that luxuries like these still took me by surprise. He showed me the pool, and a state-of-the-art kitchen, which had a fridge stocked with enough food to last us several days—caviar and champagne, various kinds of bread, and everything else I could imagine wanting. He must have sent someone ahead to prepare everything for us.

"I know you want to stand here with your mouth open, but we have more important business to take care of." He took my arm and led me into a luxury bedroom that rivaled any five-star hotel, complete with a queen-size bed covered in white silk sheets embroidered in gold, sheer curtains that danced in the breeze when the windows were thrown open, and a thick cream carpet that felt like heaven on the soles of my feet. I threw my purse onto the bed and looked at him in amusement.

"You went all out, didn't you?"

"Anything for you, my love. Now get dressed. Let's go get married."

"How are we going to get married without a minister?" I had been so entranced by the beauty around me, I had forgotten the most important part of our trip. "We need someone to officiate. I don't see a soul here but the two of us."

"Don't worry, I have everything under control. There will be someone to pronounce us man and wife. You'll meet him later. Nothing will stop me from becoming your husband today." He reached for me, and I sank into his arms. It felt good to be here, just the two of us. I'd missed it. I already felt an ache thinking about returning home, back to my fears.

We kissed for a while, our fingers tracing each other's bodies, but as he hardened against me, he pulled his lips from mine and pushed me away gently.

"Don't do this to me. Not now. We have the wedding to prepare for."

"Miles, do I even need to ask who's going to sail this yacht?" I asked before he walked out of the room.

"He's standing in front of you." He gave me a wink. "I'm a man of many talents."

"Are you serious? I don't think I know you anymore."

"Well, I guess it's time you met the other side of me." He laughed. "I'm joking. Even though I know how to handle a boat, I've hired someone for this trip. Nothing is going to keep me from spending time with you."

***

When I left the bedroom and entered the living room, Miles was waiting for me. He was dressed in a black tux, his hair shiny and swept back, all handsome and debonair. And he was all mine.

"You're beautiful." He ran his gaze down my body. "But I can't wait to rip that dress off you later."

I beamed up at him. "Why not now? You're sexy as hell. I'm so turned on right now."

"Later, babe." He smiled. "Let's do this first."

At that moment, there was a knock on the door.

"Come in," Miles called out.

The door opened. A man in his forties with mahogany skin entered. He had a scar on his cheek, dark brown eyes, and a salt-and-pepper fade. He wore a black and gold ship captain's uniform.

For a moment my heart jumped to my throat. What if he was my stalker, and he'd found his way onto the yacht to get to me? Anything was possible. No, it couldn't be him. I had to believe that. But the scar on his right cheek was a little creepy.

Breathe, Chloe. It's fine. You're safe here. Miles will protect you.

"Chloe, this is James Cantor, our ordained minister and captain. He'll marry us and issue all the documents we need."

"My pleasure." James didn't smile, but he extended his hand, which I shook. "You can call me Jim."

I nodded. "Nice to meet you, Jim."

"Let's get married." Miles grinned.

"Wait." I turned to him with a raised eyebrow. "Didn't you forget something?"

He narrowed his eyes. "What would that be, my love?"

"Don't we need witnesses?"

His palm hit his forehead. "Damn, you're right. I forgot about that." He glanced at Jim. "Can you take care of it for me?"

Jim nodded, then he walked out. It only took him about ten minutes to return, followed by two men in their mid-twenties, with Mohawk hairstyles and nose rings, cameras hanging from their necks.

"Not many people out there," Jim whispered to Miles.

Miles nodded, and while I was still taken aback by the idea of getting married in front of complete strangers, Miles introduced himself to the men. They shook his hand and mine, telling us their names were Boris and Aaron from

California. They confirmed they were over the age of eighteen and showed their identity documents to Miles and Jim.

Instead of worrying about the strangers, I focused on what was most important. As long as Miles was present, nothing and no one else mattered.

Jim folded his hands in front of him and turned to Miles. "Ready to get started?" he asked.

"Yes, let's do it," Miles said.

In the next few minutes, Jim said all the things he needed to say, and read a few verses from a Bible he'd brought with him. Then he asked us to say our vows to each other, as we had planned to. I went first.

"Miles," I started. "You have changed me in so many ways. You love me and protect me, and make me feel like the most special woman in the world. No—you make me feel as if I'm the only woman in the world. Every day I spend with you is a dream come true. I cannot wait to build a life together, to have your children. I will cherish you and be faithful to you always. I promise to love you forever and beyond."

Miles took a deep breath. "Chloe, you have no idea how long I've been waiting for you, for this... to see the happiness on your face on our wedding day. You're the woman I have been searching for. The day I found you, everything fell into place. I knew what I had to do. I had to make you my wife, to give you everything you deserve. I promise you a future you will never forget."

Jim didn't waste any more time. He pronounced us husband and wife.

I was so filled with joy, it was hard to breathe as we exchanged rings. I had never been this happy in my whole entire life. This one moment made everything else seem insignificant. I was finally Mrs. Chloe Durant.

CHAPTER TWENTY-SIX

After Jim joined us in matrimony and had us—and the witnesses—sign the necessary papers, Miles and I thanked him, Boris, and Aaron. And then they left us alone to celebrate.

Miles and I kissed for a long time, locked inside our bubble of happiness.

When my stomach let out a rumble, disturbing the atmosphere, Miles led me to the kitchen to feed me. He reached for a bottle of expensive champagne instead of food. Alcohol on an empty stomach might not have been a great idea, but we had just gotten married. We had to celebrate.

"I promise to give you some food afterward." Miles smiled. "But it would be wrong to start our marriage without a toast."

"I agree."

He produced two champagne flutes from a glass cabinet next to the fridge and filled them with the bubbling liquid. We toasted, drank, and kissed again. I tried to get my hands into his pants, the need for food already forgotten. My body begged for him. I couldn't stop my hands as they tugged his shirt from the waistband.

"It would also be so wrong to start our marriage without you know what," I whispered in his ear.

"We'll get to that soon enough. We've been waiting a long time for this day. Let's take it slow, make every second count."

"Yes, let's." I pulled away with a sigh. He was right: We didn't have to rush anything. We had three whole days to consummate our marriage, and the rest of our lives for everything else.

Miles shrugged off his tuxedo jacket and sat me down on a stool while he prepared dinner. To keep my stomach happy before the big meal, he placed a plate of finger food in front of me, which I nibbled on while sipping my champagne.

"You know," he said, "I never thought this would ever happen… not really. That someone like you would marry someone like me. I never told you this, but I was secretly terrified something would get in the way."

"Let's be glad nothing did." I picked up a green olive and popped it into my mouth. "Tell me, how were your past relationships different from ours?"

Miles stopped chopping the onions. "My

past relationships, were just placeholders. You were the one I was waiting for."

"Just as I was waiting for you, my love." I stood up and went to wrap my arms around his middle, feeling the slabs of muscle beneath my fingers. I leaned my head against the back of his neck while he continued chopping the ingredients. After a while, he turned around and buried his hands in my hair. "Don't start what you can't finish." He let me go and threw the ingredients into the pan.

"You underestimate me, Mr. Durant. I can definitely finish what I start."

He fixed his dark eyes on my face, then he guided me back to my stool. "Stay right here. I'll be done soon, then we'll move on to other things. It will be worth the wait, I promise."

"Fine, I'll hold you to that."

Our conversation was disturbed by the sound of my cell phone ringing. It was in my purse, back in the bedroom. I stood to go and get it. "I'll be right back."

As I reached for the phone, Miles came through the door and stopped me from answering. I turned the phone over in my hand as Lester's name flashed across the screen.

"Come on," Miles said, "we're only here for three days. No phone calls; just you and me. Promise?" He took my phone, switched it off, and pushed it into his pocket.

I hesitated. My euphoria from the wedding was dissipating fast and my stomach was already knotting up. How would I be able to focus for the rest of the evening? It would be so hard not to wonder what Lester wanted to tell me. He said he would only call when he had something important to tell me. And it was late, which meant it had to be something I needed to know.

Then again, I had no idea which time zone we were in. My internal clock was all messed up. It could be early evening or afternoon where he was.

But we only had three days of honeymoon before we returned home. It would also be too risky to talk to Lester with Miles around. I still wasn't ready to tell him everything yet. My confession would ruin the little time we had alone together.

"Okay. No calls while we're on this trip."

We returned to the kitchen, and Miles continued cooking, but my head was swimming with thoughts of my phone inside his pocket. Maybe I'd get the chance later, when he was sleeping, to see if Lester left a message.

Until then, I tried to force myself to relax. By the time Miles was done cooking, I was salivating from the aroma of spices and meat that wafted in the air. He had cooked chicken Alfredo with pasta and potato salad. It was a simple meal, but it meant everything to me. It was prepared with love.

During dinner, it was hard to keep our hands off each other. Our hands touched and clasped over the table, skin stroking skin. Miles touched my face, tucked a strand of hair behind my ear, and kissed me over and over. It was romantic and tender—an unforgettable meal. A dream wedding with hundreds of guests could not compete with what we had right now.

Finally, to my delight, Miles gave in to his desires, forgot about the rest of our dinner, and gathered me into his arms.

In the bedroom, he took his time undressing me, piece by piece, even though I saw the torture in his eyes, watched him fighting the urge to just rip my clothes off my body. But it was our wedding night, and he was staying true to his word about cherishing each second.

Once I lay there naked, with only the sea breeze sweeping over my skin, he undressed. His eyes never left my body. He took his clothes off so slowly, he could have been stripping.

I grinned. "Looks like you have other skills you haven't told me about."

"There's so much you don't know about me. Allow yourself to be surprised."

"I cannot wait."

He approached the bed, his eyes dark pools

of passion. I climbed under the sheets, and he did the same. My skin tingled against the starched sheets and his skin when his thigh brushed my hip. I leaned in for a passionate kiss, but he pulled away, his lips curling into a smile.

"Playing hard to get, husband? Isn't it a little too late for that?"

"Don't say a word." He positioned himself on top of me, but didn't enter me just yet. He slid my nipples into his mouth, taking his time with each one. With his mouth and tongue, he worked every sensitive spot on my body just the way I liked it.

"Your turn." I ached to have him inside me, but it was only fair to treat him as well.

"That's right; it's my turn. But I'm the one calling the shots here."

He didn't turn onto his back so I could put him in my mouth. Instead, he turned me onto my stomach and slid a hand underneath me, pulling me upward until I was on all fours. Then, just like that, he stroked into me. My breath caught from the unexpected turn of events.

"I thought…" I frowned. "I wanted to—"

"I know what you wanted to do," he whispered into my ear, "but like I said, I'm the one in charge." He pushed into me so hard that pain overrode pleasure. He pulled out suddenly, then slid into me again. I lost my balance, my face falling into the pillow. But he kept going, fucking me so hard my head and body slid in the direction of the headboard.

"You're hurting me," I murmured into the pillow, struggling but failing to push him away. Tears of disappointment soaked the expensive sheets. My head had reached the headboard, and with each new thrust from him, my forehead slammed into the engraved wood. How could he not hear it, the sound of my skull against the wood?

He kept fucking me, and I cried harder, attempting to pull away, but he was too strong for me. He pressed a hand on the back of my head and pushed my face into the pillow until I struggled to breathe.

"What the hell are you doing?" The pillow swallowed my words. "Please stop, Miles, you're hurting me."

Not a word from him. Finally, he grunted and shuddered as his orgasm gripped him. He was enjoying himself while my head felt as though it had been hit with a hammer. I gasped for air.

He released me and walked into the bathroom, slamming the door, leaving me paralyzed by confusion.

I pulled myself up on the bed, shivering with pain, with shock, unable to understand what had just happened. This was not how I had imagined our wedding night. What the hell?

The toilet flushed, and I heard the water running. Then the door flew open.

I flung myself at him. My bunched up fists pummeled his hard chest. Rage caused my temples to throb. "What the fuck's wrong with you? I told you to stop. You were hurting me."

A huge grin split his face and his eyes narrowed. He caught both my hands, shoving me away so hard I fell back on the bed, giving me a look that made me shudder. Something was wrong. Very wrong.

"I have been waiting for this moment for so long. I was being honest—I never thought it would arrive, but here we are." The grin was still on his face. His eyes were intense, a dark shade of brown I had never seen before.

"What you did was not right. This is our honeymoon. How could you do that? You just took what you wanted knowing full well I was in pain."

"You don't get it, do you?" He took a deep breath, frustrated at my lack of understanding. "See, it was *meant* to hurt."

"How can you say that?" I shook my head, tears flying everywhere. "I don't even know you right now."

"You don't know me? Are you sure about that? Look harder." He reached for a robe on the back of the bedroom door and put it on. His eyes didn't leave mine. "I don't blame you. It *has* been a long time. Thirteen years, five days, and three hours, to be exact. I've been counting."

"What...? What are you talking about?"

He pointed both thumbs at his chest. "It's me, Kelly... Alvin Jones. You thought you killed me. Well, turns out I'm not dead." He laughed. "And now it's my turn to do to you what you and your friends tried but failed to do to me."

My stomach dropped. I gripped the edge of the bed. I felt like I was falling.

He shoved a hand through his hair. "I know, I look quite different from that boy. It took a few surgeries and a lot of exercise to create this brand-new me."

"No," I whispered. Fear clawed through me, and sweat trickled down my spine. I felt like I was having an out-of-body experience. I didn't even realize when I lurched forward and vomited on the side of the bed. He didn't seem perturbed. Trembling, I swiped the back of my hand across my mouth and turned to look back at him, whishing it were all a dream. "Miles?"

"Don't call me that. Miles is gone, and Alvin is back from the dead." He sat at the foot of the bed, and I scooted as far away as I could. He didn't try to touch me, just kept giving me that sickening grin. I searched for Miles in his face, in his eyes, but the man in front of me was unrecognizable. Even the sound of his voice.

"No, no. You can't... you can't be." My mouth turned dry. "You're lying."

"No, baby. It was me all along." He cocked his head to the side. "I played the game like a master. I pretended to love you, to be the man of your dreams. I could have gone on pretending, but revenge is so much sweeter than love. Everything I did was meant to lead up to this moment. It was so much fun sending you those cards and watching you squirm with fear."

He reached into a drawer and removed a stack of envelopes. "With each card, I waited for you to tell me what you did, to confess. If you had, maybe I'd have forgiven you. But no. You lied to me each and every time."

He threw the envelopes down on the bed next to me. My heart collapsed, and my world started to spin. Words, thoughts, and memories swirled inside my head in a terrible tornado.

All this time, it was him. My fiancé, my husband, was a man who didn't exist. He was never real. He was an illusion. Fear hit my core like icy water, rendering me speechless.

He pointed a finger at me. "Seeing you like this? It's priceless. I can see the wheels turning inside your head." His mouth twisted. "Want to know why I went to all the trouble of being the best man for you? I wanted to make you happier than any man had ever made you, to give you your own fairytale and everything. For the grand finale, I wanted to see your pain when I took it all away. You're so fucking stupid, you fell for it." He pinned me with his eyes, his jaw set. "I went through a lot to get here. Everything I did was part of the grand plan to make you pay. Now do you understand why I named this yacht *Vendetta*?" He held up a hand to stop me from responding. "Does that name ring a bell, remind you of something? Does Vendet Group come to mind? Well, it doesn't exist. The merger wasn't real. What kept me busy the last few weeks were preparations for this day. I had no idea it would come so soon. By the way, eloping was a brilliant plan. I didn't have to wait until the honeymoon. I'd waited long enough already."

"You're lying. You're making it all up." I screamed and shook my head like a mad woman, gasping for breath, the smell of my own vomit shooting up my nostrils.

"You can choose to believe it or not. Doesn't make a difference to me either way. I'm here to make you pay for everything you did to me." He looked down at his wedding band. "In my wedding vows to you earlier, I promised to give you a future you will never forget. Your future is now. The *Vendetta* is your final destination, and I'm the last person you'll see before you die. But first, I'm going to make you suffer. By the time I'm done with you, you'll wish you were never born. It's best you prepare yourself."

With those words, my life as I knew it went up in flames.

THE END

Thank you for reading. If you enjoyed this book please consider writing a review, and recommend it to friends and family.

OTHER BOOKS BY DORI LAVELLE

Moments In time Series (4 books)
To Live Again Series (3 books)
His Agenda Series (4 books)